Letters *to* My Ex

Nikita Singh is the bestselling author of ten novels, including *Every Time It Rains* and *Like a Love Song*. She is also a contributing writer to The Backbenchers series and the editor of two collections of short stories, *25 Strokes of Kindness* and *The Turning Point*.

Born in Patna and raised in Indore, Nikita worked in the book publishing industry in New Delhi for a few years before moving to New York for her MFA in Creative Writing (Fiction) at The New School.

Nikita lives in Manhattan, where she does digital content and marketing for a solar energy company. You can find her on Twitter and Instagram (@singh_nikita) or on Facebook.

D1611132

NIKITA SINGH

Letters *to* My Ex

HarperCollins *Publishers* India

First published in India by
HarperCollins *Publishers* in 2018
A-75, Sector 57, Noida, Uttar Pradesh 201301, India
www.harpercollins.co.in

2 4 6 8 10 9 7 5 3 1

P-ISBN: 978-93-5277-658-0
E-ISBN: 978-93-5277-659-7

Typeset in 11.5/15 Minion Pro at
Manipal Digital Systems, Manipal

Printed and bound at
Thomson Press (India) Ltd

Dedicated to my wonderful friend Laura Duarte
Gómez, now Laura Marston.
I so admire your emotional resilience and
unwavering hopefulness.

Cheers to you and Scott!
m. 11 August 2018

'You're only given a little spark of madness. You mustn't lose it.'

– ROBIN WILLIAMS

January

I need to say this. I'm not sure you need to hear (or read) any of this, but once again, I have decided to be selfish. I'm writing this because *I* need to say this, regardless of whether *you* need to hear this or not. It's funny; I'd never thought of myself as a selfish person. Or at least I hadn't until last week. But then I ended up doing the most selfish thing I could've done to you, and even though a big part of me wants to take it all back, and for things to go back to some shade of normal, I know it's already way too late. I see it in everyone's disappointed faces every day.

Maa is livid and Papa, I think, is ... confused. I don't think he knows what to feel about the situation or how to react. But while he mostly just seems confused, there's one emotion that still makes it to the surface. You guessed it – disappointment. Maybe because I've been this perfect little daughter my whole life, I've never really experienced being a cause of disappointment. And now that I am a disappointment, I realize that I don't like it.

Also, I think they're angry and disappointed for all the wrong reasons, but that's a whole other conversation. With everything that's happened with you and me, I honestly can't even care too much about being the perfect daughter right now.

1

Abhay, I can't stop thinking about you. I wish I could tell you what happened, and why I did what I did, but even I don't know. All I know is that in that moment, surrounded by everyone we know and love, as we exchanged engagement rings, as our friends cheered, I knew I couldn't follow it through. I couldn't do this to us.

It still confuses me. Somehow, in that moment, my entire life shifted. It was as if for years and years, the spotlight had been on the two of us, our perfect love story. We were perfect from the beginning. After a few weeks of being with you, I felt like I had known you forever. And in the five years since, we had plenty of opportunities to get to know each other even better, and make new memories. It had all been very romantic, as fairy tale as it gets. But then … in that one second, the lights turned on and the rest of the world was illuminated. It all changed. I was smiling wide, but in the next moment when I turned away from everyone else and looked at you – my smile froze.

I can't explain why it happened. You were looking at me with the biggest smile on your face, and then … I didn't want any of it anymore. The focus shifted from everything my life would be to everything it would *not* be. Choosing that path meant giving up all the others. And I couldn't do it.

The moment sounds crazy even in my own head. I don't expect you to understand, and I don't care if it takes me ten pages or a hundred or a thousand, I want to put it on paper as the explanation you deserve. Closure, as they say.

Do you remember the first time we met? I fucking hated your guts. We always laughed about that. You were such a happy child, all of eighteen years, with that crazy mop of black hair, spiky and frosted at the tips – the most ridiculous thing I'd ever seen. And you walked all tall and lanky, with one shoulder always slightly lower than the other, adding to your swagger or whatever. You were never someone who just … existed. You could never have faded into the background. You took up a lot of space, always the centre of attention. That's what I hated about you. Before I came to love that about you.

It took me a long time – and you a lot of persistence – for me to *see* you, even though you were always there. Your big, overwhelming presence, overtaking everything else in the room. That stupid hair.

I still remember all of it fondly. You were on the cricket ground, smashing sixes, and I was in the stands, sitting alone, trying to get away from all the people and the noise. I couldn't have chosen a worse spot. The cricket stadium felt like a good idea to begin with, because it was completely empty when I first got there. Until you showed up with your friends, soon to be joined by a few more, and slowly, the stands started to fill up with adoring spectators. Funnily enough, I wasn't distracted by any of it. I enjoyed watching that slow procession, in between pages of my assignment. I tried not to care about it, but that didn't work. The cheering got louder and every time I looked up, there were more excited faces.

I didn't know you, but I knew *of* you. Everyone did. You were quite the legend with the ladies. I couldn't walk three steps on campus without hearing a mention of you. Corridors, classrooms, restrooms, the grounds – you were everywhere, in conversations. Then, suddenly, you were in my life.

I was perfectly fine, sitting at the stands all by myself, long after everyone else was gone. Including you, followed by all your fans. I saw you leave with them. I saw you turn around to look at me. I can't imagine what my face must've looked like. It was unexpected, our intense eye contact. It wasn't long or anything; maybe that, the quickness of it, added to the intensity. I remember it in scenes, like some cheesy movie. Scene 1: I was reading. Scene 2: I saw you laughing and walking away with your team, followed by the girls. Scene 3: You looked at me and I looked at you, and it was fleeting, and it was … hot and tingly. Scene 4: You were gone.

I remember feeling … inadequate. I never was the pretty-dresses-and-cute-shoes kind of girl. I didn't know what accessorizing was, or how to put makeup on. In all the eighteen years of my life till then, I had made it solely on my books and my thoughts and my conversations. I was always a *student*. I mean, of course, I was in school like everyone else, but even apart from that, in *my* time, I was always learning. It was all I did.

My family loved me, I had close friends, I had my books, not to mention my hopes and dreams and plans, and for the eighteen-year-old me, it was much more than I could've asked for. I'm the kind of person who thinks about these things – everything I have, what matters and what doesn't, what *should* matter and what *shouldn't*, things like that. I felt extremely fortunate for everything in my life. I was very well loved by the people I was surrounded by, and I was on my way to achieving all these dreams I had dreamed, at least in my head. I thought I would never need more, but until I met you, I never knew what I was missing out on.

You came back for me. Fresh out of a shower, your hair wet and not spiky (thank God). I didn't hear you or see you walk up to me, and your sudden appearance threw me. I saw your sneakers crawl up right above the book I was supporting on my lap. I quickly looked up and exhaled a loud *what the*. You just grinned a stupid lopsided grin and shook your head, making droplets of water fall on my face.

'Can you *not*?' My first words to you. It was perfect; it set the tone for our entire relationship, don't you think? You were always … *doing things*, being funny and loud and taking up so much space. I was always rolling my eyes and shaking my head at you, but loving you madly, regardless.

'Oops.' Another lopsided grin.

You never needed more, did you? Never needed to do more, put more effort into anything. You kind of just existed, and the world would fall at your feet. For one person, you had charm enough for ten. But I didn't fall for it. You've always maintained that you would've fallen for me regardless, but babe, trust me – if I'd given you attention from day one, you would've been over me in a week, like all the other girls. But I appreciate how you always claim the contrary.

By ignoring you, I wasn't playing power games or anything. I didn't even know what power games were, let alone how to play them. I simply hadn't been the object of a boy's fancy before and didn't know how to respond, or … be. It didn't help that I didn't like you very much. The entitled asshole with the perfect life who got everything he wanted. No thanks. I wasn't interested.

You refused to leave me alone. I felt your eyes watching me wherever I went, whatever I did. Class, cafeteria, hallways, everywhere. Every time you walked into a room, your eyes found me and kept returning to me every few minutes. And I became aware of this because ... I found my eyes doing the same. They were in love way before we were, our eyes. I remember feeling as though you were my true north. Every time I sensed you around me, my eyes would automatically redirect and locate you. Equal parts romantic and creepy. I would have it no other way. It was that intensity, that almost supernatural element, that madness that caught my attention.

Once I got to know you, it felt like I was let in on a secret. As if no one knew anything but us. We were feeling all of these emotions that no one else knew about, or would even understand, or ever experience. People tend to get cocky in love. We were the cockiest.

Oh God, we were insufferable, weren't we? Two peas in a pod, always together, making everyone else feel bad about themselves by rubbing what we had in their faces.

That day, at the stands, you refused to leave me alone. I told you repeatedly that I had an assignment deadline, but you just. wouldn't. go. away. You made yourself comfortable in the seat next to me and stretched out your legs on the chairs in front of us – no intentions of leaving. I would have moved away, but you smelled good.

We looked straight ahead, at the stadium. And I would alternate that with looking down at my books, and you, at me. In that hour that you sat with me, I looked at you and met your eyes like, twice. I didn't care if you thought I was standoffish or stuck-up or anything. But while I acted as if you sitting there didn't have any effect on me whatsoever, I remember the intensity and intimacy of it stirring something foreign in me.

It's still strange to me that the thing that stays with me the most from that day, apart from how great you smelled, is us looking at the empty stadium together while you talked. We were looking at the same thing, from the same vantage point, and I'm sure we were seeing different things, but it was the first thing we shared. In our first moments together, sitting side by side, looking at the empty stadium.

Eventually, you stopped talking so much. You just sat there with me as I read. You would say something every once in a while, and I would shrug or grunt in response, trying not to engage with the campus playboy. You said something about my handwriting and how I was scribbling on the margins of my book with a fine-tipped pen, you commented on my hair blowing in the wind and covering most of my face, you even said something about my little sighs. The amount of attention you were paying me, the intensity of it, it was overwhelming. Nothing escaped your notice.

I kept telling myself that you were up to no good, that nothing good could come out of entertaining you. And the nerd that I am, all I needed was a book and a pending assignment to keep me occupied while you continued being totally in my space.

When I finished marking up everything I needed for my assignment, I gathered all my things and stood up. You followed suit and extended your hand for me to shake.

'Do this again soon?' you asked.

I slipped all my books into my backpack and zipped up, deliberately, letting you hang. But in the end, I did shake your hand and meet your eyes. It was too much – the smell, the touch and the eyes, all together. The cumulative impact of those three things stunned me, but I contained myself the best I could.

Holding my eyes, you tilted your head. 'Is that a yes?'

'Was this fun for you?' I half-laughed, half-snorted.

'Absolutely. The most fun I've had in a long, long time.'

I rolled my eyes at that. I tried to pull my hand out of your grip but you wouldn't let me.

'I'm serious.'

'You enjoy being practically invisible to girls?' I asked.

'Of course not. But you're not just any girl. I would be honoured to be ignored by you every minute of the rest of my life,' you said with flourish.

'Oh, stop. You wouldn't remember my name this time next week.'

'False. Also, I need to know your name to forget it.'

'Fact.'

I pulled my hand away, successfully this time, and began walking away. I was literally skipping, suddenly realizing the meaning of that word. Based on your behaviour so far that day, I'd expected you to follow, but you stayed back and yelled out after me, 'You're not going to tell me?'

When I kept walking away, you yelled again, 'Oh, come on! How is that fair? I'm invested in you. You have captured my attention, possibly even my heart, and soul, if I dig real deep. Lady, wherever you go, I shall find you. Don't leave me now, I only just found you…' You continued being super theatrical, I continued to walk away.

I never turned back, but you were willing to bet that I was smiling as I walked away, and even though I never admitted this in the following five years that we were together – I was. I was smiling as you made a fool of yourself.

I smiled, but I wasn't taken. Not yet. I knew your reputation too well to want anything to do with you. And you stepped back too, so it was easy to push you out of my head. After that first time at the stands, I didn't see you around for a few days and then, out of nowhere, you were everywhere. You didn't say anything to me. As far as I could tell, you weren't following me either, but you were everywhere I was.

And our eyes kept doing their supernatural thing, finding their true north, siring a bond, something super weird/creepy like that. Then, one ordinary morning, as I juggled my books in my arms and rushed to class, preparing my leg to kick the door, you appeared out of nowhere and held it open for me. I glanced up as I thanked you, and realized it was *you*. You said hi. I said hi back.

And the rest, as they say, is history. Or it could've been, if I hadn't cut it short, for no apparent reason, and broken your heart and mine in the process.

When I remember all the good times, I can't think of a single reason big enough for us to not be together. Being away from you is a constant physical pain. A brick in the pit of my stomach, weighing me down, making me curl inwards, squeezing myself to become as small as I can.

The desire to pick up the phone right now and call you is overwhelming. I can't not be with you. I can't not see you every day, smell you around me, feel your touch, hear your laughter. It breaks my heart every time I remember our last kiss. So rushed, so customary. A see-you-later-babe goodbye kiss. We had no way of knowing it would be our last one. But *I* should've known. How on earth did I not know that mere hours later, I would decide to end our relationship forever, in front of everyone we know?

It was cruel. I have nothing to say in my defence. You did nothing to deserve this. I can't say anything to justify my actions.

Yet, I would do it again. I know it in my heart – I *need* this. I need you and me to not be together. I just … don't know *why*. Maybe it would be easier if I did, but I don't. I don't even know why I'm writing this, or if I'm ever going to find enough courage to give you this. I just know that I'm feeling too many things right now, and it's all become this huge mess in my head, like a big pile of … snakes, slithering around each other, jumbling up. I can't make head or tail of any of this. It's almost as if my own mind isn't mine anymore.

It feels like I'm on autopilot; I have no control over anything. The pain of losing you … or more accurately, willingly giving you up, is so crippling that I can barely hold pieces of myself together. The slightest nudge could break me. But somehow, my possessed brain knows what I need.

It's telling me to stick to my choice, to stay away from you, to open a Word document and bleed on paper, try to throw up all my jumbled thoughts in the form of words, collect all the disconnected facts, try to make sense of it all.

So far, I don't know what's happening. I comprehend that what I did to you was unforgivable, but if you were shocked by it, imagine what I'm going through. At least for you, it came from outside. Someone else made a life-changing decision for you. It happens all the time; you can't control other people's thoughts. But one should be able to control one's own thoughts and actions! For me, it came from within, without warning. Everything changed in one moment. No, *I* changed everything in one moment.

And yet, even though it was something I did, it feels like something that happened to me. I feel like a victim here, when I have no right to. I'm the cause of this. Everyone around us is thrown off, so many lives are affected, and I did it. I have no right to play the victim card here.

I know all this, but somehow, I also know that if you read this, you'll understand what I mean. You'll side with me. Even though I ripped your heart out of your chest, I know you will know my heart.

February

My life is a joke right now. Quarter-life crisis, leaving the love of my life at the (almost) altar in front of everyone we know and love, travelling to Europe alone following the aftermath – check, check and check. Cliché upon cliché upon cliché.

I'm sitting in this cute little teashop in Antwerp, thinking about you, missing you with every fibre in my body, writing this letter, which I'll probably never have the courage to send you. I don't even know what I'm writing about, except that I used to tell you everything, and now that we don't talk, I don't know what to do with all this information in my head. All the things I see, the streets I walk, the people I meet – nothing feels real because I don't get to share any of it with you.

And then there are five years' worth of memories that I keep remembering and replaying in my head. The happy memories make me sad now. Little by little, as I replay each of the beautiful moments I spent with you in my head now … in this light, the aftermath of the end of our relationship, I feel each of those moments slip away. They're ruined now. None of them are happy anymore; none of them make me smile. Our happy moments bring tears to my eyes. I'm losing the five amazing years that we spent together, one moment at a time.

I know what you're thinking. You think that this is all my fault; I did it to myself. I made the decision, I pulled the trigger, and trust me, I take full responsibility. Yes, all of this is my doing, but even so, it doesn't mean that I can't feel terrible about it and everything that followed. My words probably mean nothing to you now, because my actions are too far in the opposite direction from these worthless words, and I don't blame you. I wish I could make you believe me, somehow. If not today, then maybe eventually…

Anyway, after I broke up our engagement, I had to leave, because things are not good at home. I don't think Maa and Papa will ever forgive me. It doesn't help that the neighbours, distant relatives and everyone's dogs have questions and concerns regarding us. Everybody wants to be in on the big secret, get the first scoop of all the drama. Well, too bad. For anyone else to know what happened, *I* have to know first. And I still don't.

It's eating me up inside. As I walk the beautiful streets of Antwerp, and Brussels before that, and Amsterdam and London before that, I keep asking myself what the fuck I was thinking, and why I'm not trying to fix things; why I am not running to you and begging you to take me back … but I'm coming up with nothing.

I think back to everything that happened leading up to our engagement, to see if I can find something that could make sense, provide some sort of explanation. Somewhere, something went wrong, for us to break up so suddenly. If I can pinpoint it, maybe we can fix it.

I think it started when we got tired of lying to our families about our relationship. We weren't just friends.

We were never just friends, and we wanted them to know that. The five years that we'd been together, there's no way no one had a clue. I always felt that they knew, but played along with our lie, and secretly hoped for us to break up before anything needed to be done about the situation. I'm ashamed to admit that in my seemingly progressive family, caste is still such a big thing, and I know that you feel the same way about your family. It's not spoken of, and it's not like they would have objections about us being together exclusively on the grounds of caste, but who are we kidding? We know that they'd have much preferred that we found someone of our own caste.

So, when we told them, as we'd expected, they weren't happy. They weren't exactly surprised, but they also weren't happy. With each day that passed, they slowly got used to the idea of us together. While they weren't thrilled, they were resigned to the fact that we were in love, and we were going to spend our lives together. But if they were to allow us do that, they insisted that we do it the 'right' way. It's all about being normal, isn't it? Or at least *appearing* normal.

I think that was the first bump in our road. You and I, we were so in love, but we were also kids, fresh out of college, still wondering what we wanted to do with our lives, or where to begin in the immediate future. That's enough pressure already, without the newly revealed relationship status. Now we were supposed to fix a date. Plan the engagement, the wedding, the rest of our lives.

I hope I don't sound ungrateful when I say this, because I know our families love us deeply, but their involvement in our present and the future, however well-intentioned, was what first started to break us. We never saw each other just to talk, about … nothing and everything. Our secret was out; our relationship was public. Everyone had something to say about us. We were supposed to be a certain way, or at least *act* a certain way. Our movements were tracked, our time together was accounted for, every step we took was watched and counted. It was too much pressure, and I began to crack under it.

You seemed to be handling it so much better than me. You accepted the challenge and stepped up to it. As soon as we graduated from college, you joined your dad's company, started to go to work every day. It had never been your plan in life to join your dad's company. But even though you were doing it because you *had to*, in order to help out your family during a crisis, you didn't do it grudgingly. You embraced it with all you had, and went to work with fresh ideas every single day.

On top of all that, when we were sat down and all the engagement-/wedding-/life-planning was shoved down our throats, you took it so calmly, finding humour in every situation, almost as if this wasn't our future on the line. I don't know how you did it. Maybe you were just letting them have their 'fun' and were unbothered by the pressure it put on us, but honestly, it felt to me sometimes as if you simply did not care.

You found fulfilment in your job, and happiness in your new friends at work. You would come home and laugh off all the life-planning. I wish I could've been more like you. Because I struggled every second of every day, inside my own head, trying to figure out what I wanted to do with my college degree. It's been almost a year since we graduated college, and I still don't know what I want to do with my degree. Studying political science and planning to save the world is one thing. But after college, when it was actually time for me to do something, begin somewhere, I felt completely lost (and still do). I would work, browse through jobs all day, trying to find the 'best fit', since that's what everyone was talking about. It was hard for me to find this fit, because I first had to know who I was and what I wanted, before finding something that would fit my requirements. Confused about what I wanted to focus on, I sent out applications for everything to everyone. I thought having some real options would make it easier for me to pick one, but my brilliant plan backfired terribly. As I started interviewing, the options on the table only made me more and more confused. Not that I had job offers flooding my inbox, but the ones I did have…

It wasn't enough. None of it was enough. Working for a non-profit organization, in a small capacity somewhere, wouldn't make enough of a difference. It would be years, probably decades, before I'd be able to make an impact on anything or anyone. But I had to start somewhere. Maybe I wouldn't be happy with it immediately, but I would learn to love it, right?

And then there were the other questions we used to talk about. Does it make more sense to work on the ground level and make a small amount of difference every day? Or would we make more of an impact if, instead of working for a small NGO somewhere, we were to get a hot-shot high-paying job and give back? Money does make the world go round.

Either way, I wasn't going to be able to do a whole lot right out of college, and patience never has been one of my stronger suits. And then there is the question that always haunted me (it still does): how do I choose the one thing I would do, when doing that would mean I don't get to do all the other things I won't do? Every time I think of a decision that would close doors, I panic. I couldn't see a clear path ahead of me, and the uncertainty and insecurity was taking a big toll on me.

When everything else seemed to be falling apart, I can't explain how it made sense to ruin the one good thing in my life. We, you and I, always worked. Then why did I have to destroy that?

I sometimes wonder why it was that we worked so well. Could it be because we never actually faced a real problem? I'm not saying that we haven't gone through anything together, because we know that that's not true. We've both gone through some really tough times together. But this... this was different. Our entire world shifted; nothing was the same. After college, our routines, our every day, the places we went, the people we saw, the situations we were in – all of it was new. Nothing was familiar.

Please tell me how you dealt with it, because I really wasn't handling it well. I began to understand what people meant when they said that they felt the walls around them closing in on them. That is a very accurate way to describe how I felt in my own home. Sitting in my room, hunched over my laptop, trying to find work that would bring me some sort of satisfaction at the end of the day, I could almost physically feel the tension on the other side of the door.

Papa verbally expressing his displeasure about having to 'deal with' your dad for the engagement/wedding arrangements. Maa trying to keep him calm but also quietly angry with me for putting them in this position in the first place, by falling in love with you. Bhaiya trying to not lose his shit, as he explained to them that this is 2016 and we should probably let go of all this caste nonsense and try to get along for the sake of my happiness.

It was as if I'd stepped into a cheesy '90s movie, with the family and society drama stopping us from being together. Quite honestly, it was ridiculous. When you distance yourself from it, it was hilarious, wasn't it? But that's perhaps where the problem lies. That you were able to distance yourself from it, while I got caught up in every word that was said. They wouldn't leave my mind, hours after they were said, even when they weren't that serious.

I have two complaints from myself. 1) I want a weaker memory, so I can let things go. I don't *enjoy* overthinking everything, or holding grudges, or stressing out over little things, or losing sleep. But I don't have a choice. Because I remember every fucking thing anyone ever said, and can never just move the fuck on. And 2) I need to be less of a control freak. I don't do so well in situations that aren't 100 per cent under my control. I want every single aspect of my life to be perfect, all the time. This is not ideal.

I couldn't just be okay with some people not liking each other. It was okay that my dad wasn't a fan of your father. They got along alright, they were cordial with each other, they didn't need to be best friends. But I got obsessed with needing everyone to get along with everyone else all the time, and it's as exhausting as it sounds. Things kept going wrong, one after another, and while by the time we got to our engagement, everyone was being amicable, I remembered every word that had been said in the past. I noticed every slight pursing of lips, every twitch of an eye and it drove me insane. (Which could be a partial explanation; I have to be at least partially insane for having broken off our engagement, right?)

On that day, when you arrived at the venue, looking every bit as charming as you had the first time I realized I had fallen in love with you, all I wanted to do was run away from you. Leave everyone and everything behind, especially you, and never look back. Find myself a new life. I agree that a big part of it was the family and society stuff, but that wasn't all.

I know what it was. I'm afraid to say it because once I do, it becomes real. I don't want it to be real … and I know the first thing you will say, but please hear me out first. The reason I had to leave was because I knew, and it had become clearer and clearer to me in the months leading up to the engagement, that you didn't love me anymore.

Your first instinct to this is that I'm absolutely wrong, isn't it? I don't blame you. Anyone who knew us, all of our friends, they would all agree with you. You clearly adored me. Your world revolved around me. You were always so warm and kind and made me laugh constantly. Things were perfect, right?

Only, when was the last time it was just the two of us and you were still warm and loving and made me laugh? It felt as if, in front of everyone else, you were on autopilot. You were at a 100: happy, funny. You used up all your charm on this show that we put up for them to see. And by the time it was just us, you were exhausted, and just wanted to … not do any of that. You didn't have anything left to give me. I don't blame you for it, we were both under a lot of pressure and were dealing with it differently, but it did take a big toll on our relationship. Because while you just wanted to avoid talking about any of that when we were together (or anything else for that matter), I, on the other hand, waited for us to be alone, so that I could talk to you, tell you things, hold your hand, touch your lips.

One might argue that it could've just been a phase, but Abhay, we were twenty-three. This is a phase people end up in after they've been married for decades and have kids and responsibilities and life to worry about. How did we end up there? And more importantly, how did it not bother you?

I was so close to you, then how did I still miss you so, so much?

Then that day, all of a sudden, you were standing next to me, holding my hand, sliding the ring on my finger, beaming at a cheering crowd, while I ... I can't even say it. It sounds pathetic when I talk about it. But considering that I'm probably never sending you this letter, I don't lose a whole lot by saying it.

During our engagement ceremony, on the stage, I kept looking at you, trying to catch your eye, but you were looking at everyone *but* me. You were caught up in the moment – the slaps on your back, the loud cheers, the cameras, the ... happiness. Wasn't *I* supposed to be the reason for your happiness? I could've disappeared from the scene in that moment, and you wouldn't even have noticed. That's how I felt. I felt that small, that insignificant, standing next to you on that stage. Should I have felt like that when I was about to get engaged to the love of my life?

Once the cheers faded and our friends stopped their drunken hooting and clapping, you turned to me, only because it was my turn to put the ring on your finger. I was still looking at you, and when your eyes met mine, mine were brimming with tears. My entire world was falling apart inside me. As soon as our eyes met, mine flooded and tears began to fall unchecked. I was so embarrassed, angrily wiping them off my cheeks.

I can understand why everyone else would think that I was just emotional or *aww how cute, she's crying.* But I don't think I can forgive *you* for not knowing immediately that something was terribly wrong. I was breaking inside. Every cell in my body was screaming for your attention, your love, your affection, but you couldn't even *see* me, could you?

That was the moment I *knew*. I couldn't marry a stranger, and that's what you had become. Honestly, I was surprised that you even put up a fight when I was leaving. I'd half expected the party to go on without me after I left the stage. That's how worthless I felt. And I don't care if it's unfair to you, but I blame you for it. My eyes were only searching for yours, but even when you looked directly at me, I couldn't find what I was looking for. This person, standing next to me, making promises of commitment ... he was a stranger. I didn't know you at all.

It's like they say in the movies – I saw it happen as if in third person. I felt myself leave my body and look at everything that was happening. I saw myself pull my hand away. You laughed, assuming I was just joking. You caught my hand again and pulled me closer to you, laughing even louder. *I couldn't take it.* We were in entirely different worlds. We were so disconnected from each other; you were completely clueless to what I was feeling.

I saw myself pull my hand away again, this time more forcefully, unable to hide my anger. I can't think of a time I had been angrier at another person, or myself. It suddenly felt like a business transaction, all of it. I was disgusted. We were going through the motions, doing things we were supposed to do, like robots. Signing a contract to live together for the rest of our lives. *I just couldn't do it.*

When I pulled my hand away a second time, I did it more forcefully, with more finality. I looked you directly in the eye, and through the hot tears, whispered, 'I can't do this.'

That was your first clue, and even then, you looked confused. We were on such different planets by then that even when I was breaking down in the middle of our engagement ceremony, in front of everyone, you had no idea what was going on.

I felt the force of all of it together as I stumbled away. People calling out to me, all the questions, the steps that followed me. I was so angry and so, so disappointed with us, for letting our love come to this. With each step that I took away from that stage, it felt more and more like I was escaping a life sentence. If I was truly marrying the love of my life, I would imagine it would feel quite different from that. It should've been the happiest day of my life – getting engaged to marry you. Then why did walking away lift such a heavy weight off my shoulders? Why did I suddenly feel like I could breathe again?

Leaving behind the million questions, murmurs and confused and angry faces, I grabbed my handbag and car keys. At that moment I felt lighter than I had in months. You followed me. You caught up with me just as I was about to walk out the door, and demanded an explanation.

You know what hurt the most? The look in your eyes – it wasn't sadness. It wasn't even confusion. It was anger, plain and simple. What did you think was happening? That I was following a script, just for entertainment? How could you not know that it was killing me to walk away from you?

You were angry with me as if I was an unreasonable child acting against your (or our families') wishes. That first look you gave me was pure rage.

'Where are you going?' you demanded, grabbing my arm.

'Away from all this.' It wasn't an explanation, and I owed you one, so I stopped and turned to face you. I looked up at you, and said, 'You don't love me anymore. We shouldn't be together.'

I didn't need to say much more. All three of those sentences were true, and described in a nutshell exactly how I was feeling or what I was doing. And that was enough for you to understand, at least a little, why I was leaving.

I saw your face change. I saw the anger leave, and you let out a troubled breath, opening your mouth to say something … but then closing it without letting any words escape. I could tell that your mind was racing, trying to find explanations, excuses, something. But you came up with nothing. You wanted me to stay; your grip on my arm established that. But you couldn't think of a single reason *why* I should stay.

You said zero words. I was leaving you, and you said nothing to stop me.

Was that acceptance? Did you agree that you didn't love me anymore, and that we shouldn't be together and I should get away from all of that? If you didn't agree, why didn't you say something? Anything. I just needed you to tell me that I was wrong. That you did love me. That's all I needed to know.

I thought that I was too far gone, my foot literally out the door, but one word from you and I would've stopped. I would like to think that my decision was final and I wasn't going to change my mind, but who am I kidding? It's you;

when it comes to you, I do unreasonable things. I would've stayed with you forever, if you'd asked me once.

But you couldn't find a single word to say to me. Not one word.

You stood there and watched me get into the car, still wiping the stubborn tears off my face. I watched you watch me, in the rear-view mirror, and my heart fell heavy into my stomach. Standing there at the door, watching me leave, your arms at your sides, shoulders hunched in sadness, and the pain on your face...

I will never forgive myself for causing that. I will try to forgive you for not saying a single word as I drove away.

March

From: Abhay Shukla
Sent: 23/3/2017 4:40 PM
To: Nidhi Sharma
Subject: I need to say this

Nidhi,

Since you won't take my phone calls or respond to my texts, this is the only way I can think of reaching you without you calling the police on me. I must say, it's kind of crazy how quickly you went from not being able to imagine a life without me to this. You see me on the street and you immediately turn the other way, as if you never knew me.

I know you're angry, for many different reasons, and somehow, at the moment, all of it is directed exclusively towards me. That's okay; it's your prerogative. You're allowed to feel whatever it is you're feeling. So, if you don't want to talk to me, or even see my face without cringing, that's okay. You don't have to. But I do need to get this off my chest, so I will leave this in your inbox and so you have the option to read it if/when you so please.

We broke up. *You* broke us up. It was *your* decision to end things, I was not involved in any of the planning or decision-making and my wishes were definitely not considered in this decision that affected my entire life. But okay. If one person out of the two doesn't want a relationship, it dies right then and there. I couldn't force you to stay with me when you so clearly didn't want to. I accepted that as you literally ran away and left me behind.

But won't you agree that since we are not together anymore, it's okay for me to find someone else? Has the mourning period passed? Am I allowed to rebuild my life now? Or should I just go crawl into a hole and die? Is that what you'd like to see? Or do you just not care at all?

Well, considering your reaction today when you saw me walking out of that store with Piya, you do care. Was it the fact that I didn't look absolutely miserable, or that it was Piya I was with, or just that I am still alive that bothered you the most?

I don't owe you an explanation at all, but because I'm still human, and I still care about you (my feelings don't switch off in a split second like yours, you see) I will tell you this — you can relax. There's nothing going on between Piya and me. She got that job that Dad got her an interview for, so she wanted to meet up and thank me over coffee. Again, in the interest of honesty,

I do think she likes me. But I don't think it's a big deal, and I'm sure it's just a fleeting emotion. As far as my feelings towards her are concerned, there aren't any.

As much as I'd like to move on, I can't feel anything about anyone, even if I tried. I don't know if I ever will. When I try to imagine a time where I would be able to place all of my faith in another human being, and trust them with everything I have, I simply cannot see it happening again.

I gave you everything I had, every piece of me was yours, but you didn't want it. It seemed like you did, you know, when you told me a thousand times that you loved me, and wanted to build a life with me and couldn't imagine living without me. When we fought everyone and everything that came in our way in order to be together, but then, it turned out that you didn't actually want any of that.

Anyway, I have thought about this for days and weeks and months at end and haven't been able to find an answer. I'd be lying if I said I wasn't expecting you to give me one. When you left, even as you were breaking my heart, I *knew* that there was a reason. I know that you didn't just do it for no reason at all. And I *knew* that one day you would tell me why. It's been three months now, and you spin on the spot and go the other way when you see me, so I'd be an idiot to expect any kind of honesty, or any words at all from you.

Lastly, and I won't take too much of your time with this, but I do need to tell you that I'm angry too. With you. I don't fully understand what happened that day. I can think of a few reasons why you were unhappy with the way things were. However, even after having thought about this a *lot*, I can't think of something so big and unresolvable that would make you decide to immediately end everything. I know that things were stressful at home. They were stressful for me too. But I was dealing with it. I could see that at the other end of this would be *us*, together. All that mattered to me was that we would be with each other and everything would go where it was supposed to. But that was clearly not what mattered to you.

I'm sorry if I'm being aggressive in this email. I understand that if I'm unhappy with the way I expressed something, I can easily edit it. But I won't, in the interest of honesty. I'm not pleased with how I expressed some things in this letter, but I honestly feel this way, so I'm presenting you the unadulterated version of the truth.

Also, I didn't mean to sound this formal. But considering how I feel as if I don't know you at all anymore, it's quite fitting.

I don't know how to close this. I have no expectations from you.

Hope you're happy.

Abhay

*

From: Nidhi Sharma
Sent: 23/3/2017 5:33 PM
To: Abhay Shukla
Subject: RE: I need to say this

I have no right to expect anything from you, I know that. After what I did, the last thing I can demand is that you follow my wishes. Or anything, actually. I can't make any demands at all.

It was good to hear from you. I know, I know. It was hardly a love letter, but I'm still glad you wrote to me, because I certainly didn't have the courage to initiate this very important, long-overdue conversation. I still don't know what to tell you, or how to begin this. There are so many things I have to say to you. And now that I am writing this, it's hard to know where to begin.

First things first, I owe you an apology for behaving the way I did when I saw you at the coffee shop today. And also for being too much of a coward to take your phone calls. That's exactly what it is: I'm a coward. When I saw you walking out of the shop, I hadn't expected to see you, and it happened so suddenly, I was taken aback. I know that's no excuse for turning on my heels and running away, but it is the truth. In the months that we've been apart, I have imagined us crossing paths again in various different scenarios. Maybe at a mutual friend's party somewhere, or somewhere randomly, like today. But I hadn't expected to be taken so off guard when it actually happened.

I would be lying if I tried to pretend that my reaction had nothing to do with the fact that you were with that girl. I don't know her at all, but I'm sure she's lovely. I believe you when you say there's nothing going on between you two, and I can definitely believe that she likes you. I appreciate you telling me all this, but it's not like you owe me an explanation. I don't deserve anything from you.

Of course, you are right in expecting an explanation from me. Only a monster would do what I did and give you no closure of any sort. I have been meaning to talk to you. And trust me, I have been trying to find a way to explain to you what happened and why. But every time I think about it (which is all the time) my thoughts keep going around in loops, circling over and over again till I lose track of the head or tail of it and everything stops making sense (not that there was a lot of sense to begin with).

I guess what I'm trying to say is — I've been struggling to provide you an explanation, because I don't have one. You were shocked and confused by someone else's sudden change of mind. I was too. Only, it was my own mind that shocked and confused me. I don't understand why I did what I did, except that deep down I honestly believed that something about us was broken irreparably, and I couldn't fix it.

I have nothing to tell you. The fact that this decision came from my mind didn't allow me an inside scoop of the reasoning behind it. If anything, maybe you have a better idea than me; you were always able to read my mind, remember? You always knew what was going on, or how I felt about something even before I did. So, you tell me — what happened to us?

I can't believe what I'm doing, posing this question to you, when I'm the one who owes you the answer. But, Abhay, I have racked my brain — trying to make sense of this, to arrive at some sort of a closure — and found nothing. My head is foggy, my heart is sore, it hurts everywhere, all the time.

I walk around not knowing where I'm going, and end up in places I don't recognize. I've travelled to the ends of this city; wherever the metro would take me. Just to get away from home, and everyone I've disappointed, I walk aimlessly, not knowing what to do with myself and my time. It's like I'm on autopilot (and not a very good one, considering that not once have I found myself somewhere I was pleased to be).

And then, today, my autopilot took me to you, and I was jolted back to reality. After the initial shock of coming face to face with you. When my eyes met yours, and we stopped dead in our tracks. All my thoughts halted. The entire world came to a pause. It was just your eyes holding mine. There was no sound, no movement, no air. And then I was flooded with feelings all at once. I didn't know what to do. Walk up to you and talk to you?

What would we have talked about? What would you have said? *What are you doing here? How have you been? Why did you run away and leave me?* I had answers to none of those questions. So, I took the easy way out again. It wasn't easy at all, actually, but compared to the alternative, it was sufferable.

I hope you find at least some kind of relief in knowing about my suffering. You deserve the satisfaction. You deserve so much more. I wish I could give you everything, but I can't even give you a simple answer.

I'm sorry, Abhay. I really don't have more answers for you. I wish I did, but this is all I have. I'm sorry that this is disappointing. People should expect disappointment from me at this point.

N

*

From: Abhay Shukla
Sent: 23/3/2017 6:07 PM
To: Nidhi Sharma
Subject: RE: I need to say this

No, I derive no pleasure from knowing about your suffering. Don't you know me at all? Who do you think I am? In the three months that we've been apart, yes, I have hated you on various occasions and hoped for a lot of things, but seeing you suffer like you say you are was never one of them.

Yes, it is unfair of you to ask me to explain to you why you did what you did. This question has been eating me up inside for months. I too have imagined multiple scenarios where this would make sense. Nothing ever clicked.

When I put my feelings aside, remove myself from the equation and inspect this situation, I still come up with nothing. I'm trying to believe you when you say that you *know* you have a valid reason, even though you don't know what it is. From the years that I've known you, I trust you enough to know that you do have a reason.

I also know that you loved me. And that you wouldn't throw away everything we held so dear, for absolutely no reason. That just doesn't make sense; there has to be a reason.

If you ask me, I still believe that there wasn't a reason big enough, a problem irreversible enough that we couldn't have been together anymore. We're both fairly reasonable humans; I believe we could've found a way. If both of us tried; but you didn't want to.

Going back to the big question, the only thing that I can think of that was big enough ... is the one thing we decided never to speak of again. However, since we have already lost everything, I guess there's nothing more to lose now.

So ... could the reason underlying this be that incident with Anamika? I might be way off on this, especially since it happened over a year ago, but it's the only thing I can think of that was a line that was crossed, and is irreversible.

I know that the damage caused by that break of trust was irreversible, but I thought that we controlled it as much as we could. I wanted to talk about it, and explain to you exactly what happened and that it didn't mean anything or change how I feel about you, but you insisted we don't talk about it, move on from it and never bring it up again.

It's the one thing we glazed over and never resolved. For weeks, even months after the incident, there was a visible change in the way we were with each other. Something broke, and the crack has been visible ever since. Initially it saddened me, and I didn't think we were ever going to go back to normal again, but then we did. At least I thought we did.

Because we never talked about it, and because we are talking about it now, for the first time, I need to tell you something I thought about a lot during those days. Please know that I am not trying to justify my actions. I still take the entire blame for this. All I'm trying to do is explain it from where I stand...

The way I see it, there are two types of cheating. There's one where one person knowingly steps out of a committed relationship, lies, covers his tracks, plans his moves in order to continue lying. It's like a lifestyle, a conscious decision to cheat. The other is a mistake. Nothing more.

Reality is messy. It's not as cut and dried, but if I can promise you one thing, it's that the kiss between

Anamika and me was a mistake. I didn't plan it, I wasn't attracted to her and acting on an impulse or anything. It was an office party, everyone was drinking, we stepped out to say bye to a couple of colleagues and she kissed me.

I accept that I didn't resist. That's on me. I was surprised, and confused. I didn't fully understand what was happening ... but I didn't resist.

I take all of the blame for that. If I could go back and change things, I would. Without a second thought, I would do things very differently. It was the most terrible, unimaginably hurtful thing I have ever done to you, and for that I will never forgive myself. We were so in love. I couldn't think about anything or anyone else, until all of a sudden, someone else was kissing me and I didn't stop it. It threw me off too.

Will you believe me, please, please will you believe me when I tell you it didn't mean anything?

I have gone back to that moment a hundred times, looking for an answer. Why didn't I stop it... Things between you and me hadn't been so good. We weren't carefree college kids anymore, things were changing. We were both changing, growing ... and growing apart. We could see that. Our lives had less and less in common every day. But it never got that bad ... bad enough for me to look outside of us. And I didn't! Please, please trust me — I didn't want anyone else.

Nothing more happened between Anamika and me, on that night or after. I had no feelings for her that night, or after. I loved you and only you. I know that people tend to compare, in shitty situations like this, but there was no comparison between how I felt about you and how I felt about her. Because my feelings towards her have always been non-existent.

I wish I had told you this then. I should've made sure you knew. I should've insisted I told you how much I loved you, and how much I regretted betraying your trust. I would've done anything to earn it back. I would've spent every second of every day trying to make it up to you, and earning back your trust. Before it was too late...

There. I think this is the skeleton in our closet that resulted in us ending. Or at least, this is my best guess. This is what broke us. We never talked about it. I never explained it, and you never knew how I felt. I wonder if things had turned out differently for us and we would have had a much stronger relationship if I had insisted that we discuss it and resolve it, instead of pushing it under the rug. I'm not saying that I could've gotten you to trust me a hundred per cent again, but I should've ensured that I did everything in my power to bring you as close to it as I could. I regret not trying harder. I was too scared to bring it up; I didn't want to lose you. I wish I had been brave then, because I lost you anyway, didn't I?

Abhay

*

From: Nidhi Sharma
Sent: 23/3/2017 11:29 PM
To: Abhay Shukla
Subject: RE: I need to say this

Hey, can we meet for a coffee tomorrow?
N

*

From: Abhay Shukla
Sent: 23/3/2017 11:31 PM
To: Nidhi Sharma
Subject: RE: I need to say this

Yes. Noon, same place as always?
Abhay

*

From: Nidhi Sharma
Sent: 23/3/2017 11:32 PM
To: Abhay Shukla
Subject: RE: I need to say this

See you then.
N

April

I'm going to write down everything we talked about today. I believe it's very important that I document everything I remember from today. Feelings have a tendency to pass with the moment, or morph into something else, or even change completely with time. I want to remember today exactly how it happened, the way I feel right now. Because maybe next week or month or year, when I look back at it, I would see the same incident differently. I know, I know – perspective is important, and definitely helps in the long run, but in this case, I don't want perspective to change my memory of my time with you today. I want to preserve the moment as I felt it when it was happening.

Let me begin by reiterating that I was glad you wrote to me yesterday. I couldn't find the courage to call you, or take your calls, and we saw what happened when I was face to face with you, so a letter from you gave me a better opportunity to express myself. I'm not sure I was helpful, or if my words made any sense to you. But it led to our meeting today, and I'm glad I got to see you.

You were already waiting for me when I got to the café. I was a few minutes early too, and for some reason, when I saw you sitting inside through the glass window, I paused, strategically positioned myself so you couldn't see me if you looked up … and watched you. Not in a creepy way though (or maybe in a creepy way). I hadn't seen you in three months, after seeing you every day for several years (the encounter yesterday where I saw you for three seconds and then panicked and fled doesn't count) and it was comforting just to watch you with your coffee.

If you were nervous at all, it didn't show. You looked calm and collected – the opposite of how I felt. I wasn't just watching you from outside to be a creep; I needed a few minutes to compose myself. Just seeing you brought tears to my eyes. I had to take a moment to pull myself together before going in.

I was so very nervous. When I checked my reflection in the window, I could see the stress show in the dark shadows under my eyes and the stiffness of my jaw. Ever since I left you, I have acquired this sadness that shows constantly on my face. There's nothing you could pinpoint that has changed specifically. It just looks like … in the months that we have been apart, I have aged a few years. Or it could just be me; maybe the untrained eye cannot notice the difference.

When I finally walked into the coffee shop, you looked up and spotted me immediately. My heart fluttered. I know, I know. I'm not supposed to be feeling things for you anymore. I'm trying to stop. It's probably going to take a while. Despite what you think, I don't have a switch that magically turns off my feelings either.

I wish I hadn't been shaking so badly when I walked in and you got up to say hi. We smiled at each other, but neither of us *smiled*. Your eyes looked so pained. I felt a tinge of regret, looking at you, at all I have lost.

'Hey,' you said, the forced smile on your face lingering.

'Hey, you,' I said, as I dropped my bag on the floor and pulled a chair across from you. It was strange not to … touch you. I can't remember the last time I greeted you without a kiss on the cheek or a hug. But neither of those things seemed appropriate anymore, and a handshake would've just made me sad. Things have changed so much.

'Was there traffic coming here?' you asked. Your hair was dishevelled, as if you had been running your fingers through them. I wondered if you had been nervous about seeing me too.

'Always. I swear to God, I'm *this* close to physically hurting someone for honking. The entire road is jammed, there's absolutely nowhere for anyone to go, what's honking gonna achieve?' I said, happy for something to talk about. 'Idiots on the road, I tell you. Plus, the smoke and the pollution, not to mention the heat. I was so claustrophobic in the car, but I couldn't even crack open a window. What a complete nightmare.'

You were quiet, but I noticed a slow smile creep up the corners of your lips. I counted that as a small win.

'What! I'm serious,' I continued blabbering. 'I can't believe how hard it's become for a person to go from point A to point B in this city. All of this is ridiculous.'

At this point, you smiled openly. I felt warmth flow through my body. I was instantly less nervous, but for some reason, I was too hot but also chilly at the same time. It was the strangest experience. I didn't get much of a chance to ponder over it, because you finally spoke.

'Sounds like there was traffic coming here,' you said.

'Really? What gave it away?' I laughed. The two-second pause freaked me out, and I quickly filled it with, 'What about you? Did you encounter traffic coming here too?'

'Yes, but not half bad as you, clearly.'

'Or maybe just as bad as me. I tend to exaggerate, remember?'

I immediately regretted saying that. I didn't even think about it till the words had already left my mouth. We can't make personal jokes anymore; neither can we talk about the past as if our relationship with each other hasn't changed. I can no longer casually bring up moments we'd shared when we were still together.

You nodded wordlessly.

This time, I didn't fill the silence with words either, so it grew between us. We were both unprepared for the conversation that was to follow, but it had to happen. There was no more beating around the bush. After the uncomfortable pause, in which I struggled to find a way to start talking again, you spoke.

'Was I right?' you asked.

'I don't know,' I said quietly.

Your frustration showed on your face. 'I'm sorry, but I will not accept that response. You can't say that to everything. We need answers. You owe us answers.'

I nodded, gulping hard, trying to form words. 'I think...' I began, still struggling to form the right words in my head before speaking, 'I think, yes, it was part of the reason.'

You were quiet for a long time. So was I. I had thought about this all night, and for months before that. You know this was the one incident in our life that I wanted to completely erase. Never evaluate, never wonder about. That was the only way I knew I could move on and we could be okay. But we broke up anyway. So maybe you're right. Maybe we should have talked about it, tried to resolve it.

'Why didn't you tell me?' you asked, your voice low. 'If this was hurting you ... if it was so unbearable that you couldn't imagine sharing your life with me anymore, why didn't you tell me?'

'I didn't want to think about it.'

'But you were.'

'I was.' I nodded, ever so slightly. Yes, I thought about it. Not consciously; I would never allow myself to think about it actively. But it was always in the back of my mind. Literally 24x7. It existed in my subconscious mind, a string of weed growing inside my brain, uninvited, unwelcome, thriving.

'You should've said something.' I couldn't bear to see the look in your eyes.

'I should've.'

'Are you going to say something now?' I could feel your frustration rising. I didn't blame you.

'Yes,' I said, even though I really, really didn't want to talk about it. It was clear that you needed me to, and I had been so incredibly selfish before, I couldn't do it to you again. So, I began speaking again, 'I thought … I thought that if we pretended that it never happened, it would disappear. Not immediately, but eventually. I thought we could try to move on from the stupid mistake, leave it in the past and never think about it again. Just completely erase that one minute from our life, as if it had never happened.'

You waited. My head worked frantically to gather thoughts and form words, somehow package my haphazard emotions in a box, so that it would make sense.

I gulped again, and began, my voice breaking, 'When you told me, it was as if I was thrown in ice-cold water. I felt the shock reverberate through my entire body. I couldn't think. My head was so foggy, my stomach so heavy. I couldn't make head or tail of it. None of it made sense. You were my everything. Never had I ever thought…' I trailed off, shaking my head, as I thought back to that night. You'd warned me that you had something important to tell me, but I wasn't even nervous. If there was a problem, big or small, we would solve it, we always did. There was no reason for me to be nervous. I didn't even think about it.

I remember you looking at me with fearful eyes. During the entire drive, you kept shooting me nervous sideways glances. I kept joking about how you were freaking me out, and filling your nervous silence with chatter about my day. When you told me, you made sure you had my full attention, something people would do when breaking the news of a close one's death. You knelt down in front of my chair and held both my hands in yours. Your fingers were shaking, your entire body was. That was my first clue that something was seriously wrong.

Even before you said the words, tears started streaming down both our eyes. I could sense that I was going to be exposed to immense pain. I knew this was going to be bad, that it was going to hurt us both. Then you began talking, mixing facts with feelings. *She kissed me, I swear I didn't know she liked me, I had no idea, I didn't give her any signals.* At that point, even though I was hurt, I was mostly angry with her. My dormant violent tendencies were coming to the surface. I wanted to punch her. I wanted to physically remove her from you. In the first few seconds, I went from being shocked, to hurt, to angry, to thinking that this could eventually become a funny story. Something we'd look back upon years later. Remember that one time that one girl kissed you and I went over there and kicked her ass?

I remember wondering for a second why you were behaving as if life as we knew it was changing, or the world was ending, if this was just a funny story to tell our kids someday.

Then you told me the part that killed me.

And it all made sense, even as none of this was making any sense. *I didn't resist. In the beginning, I was taken aback, but I didn't do anything to stop it.* My mind was flooded with questions. *Did you like it? Did you kiss her back? Do you like her?* I didn't ask any of those questions out loud. I couldn't bear to hear the answers.

You kept talking, answering all of my unasked questions, and I could tell that you were trying to make sense of it just as much as I was. The world stood still, as we sat together that night, completely shaken. Hours and hours later, we agreed that *it was just a kiss, it didn't mean anything or change anything*. And that's what I tried to hold on to, for the days and weeks to follow.

'I know there's no point discussing any of this now … I thought we could move past it and treat it as a one-time mistake that didn't matter at all and nothing would change, but it did, Abhay. Nothing was the same afterwards. Everything shifted. I couldn't stop thinking about it, and wondering. It affected everything. Our friends would talk about how great you and I were together, and I would think about that night. I would read articles about relationships and betrayal and I would think about that night. We would be together, walking down the street, and I would look at you and think about that night. That's all I did, all the time. It consumed me,' I said. 'Every second of every day.'

'I wish you had told me.'

'You think I never thought about that? What good would that have brought, dragging you into this emotional hell with me? A world of circular thoughts, spiralling over and over until none of it made any sense? I came up with so many theories to explain everything. Trying to box it up neatly and put it away. I guess that's the problem when it comes to decisions made by someone else's mind. You can't completely know the reasons and motivations behind them, so you can't justify or conclude anything.'

'You could've asked me anything. I would've told you. This is…' You shook your head, as if unable to find words. 'You know I would've told you anything. I would've done anything to help you through this… Why didn't you let me?'

I wanted to make it easy for you. 'If you think that this was a missed opportunity … I don't know, something that we could've talked about and resolved. I disagree. Something broke, and it changed my entire world-view. I doubted everything. Everything you did or said … I couldn't trust you like I did before. I honestly don't believe that the damage was reversible.'

'How can you be so sure? How could you have had so little faith in us?' Apart from the obvious disappointment, I sensed some of your anger coming back too.

'It was because of the nightmares,' I told you, looking away. 'Even if I was able to survive the day, pushing the recurring thoughts to the back of my head and not letting them win… I would be fine for days, but then I would wake up in the middle of the night with terrible nightmares, back to square one. I couldn't control them. It got so bad that I would try to stay up all night, to a point where I got so tired that I would just pass out and end up in an uneasy, dreamless state. I would wake up exhausted, and go through my day in a zombie-like state, but it was better than the nightmares…'

'Nidhi … why didn't you tell me any of this? I don't know what to say, or how to help you, or this situation…' you said, still shaking your head. I could see you struggle with processing this information. Were you trying to think back to the last months of our relationship, to align everything you knew with everything you just found out?

I slapped the table and sat back, physically trying to shake myself out of those thoughts and memories. 'There's no point talking about this now. It's too late, it's not going to help anything. That's why I didn't want to say anything. The past is the past, all of this has already happened. Talking about it, living in it, I don't see how it can help either of us. And again, *I* have to deal with it, and I have been dealing with it, but why would I make you go through it too? That doesn't sound fair at all.'

'What are you talking about? It's not fair to you!' You looked exasperated. '*I* am the reason behind this. I caused this. If anyone has to face the repercussions—'

'Okay, enough,' I said with finality. 'I don't have a choice, but you can be saved from all this needless misery. Besides, there's no point diving into all this shit now, so let's just not, okay? I'd much rather not.'

You were quiet. You were clearly agitated, but quiet, until you whispered, 'You're doing it again. Shutting me out.'

It was my turn to be exasperated. 'Because there is no point!' I said, louder than I'd intended. All my emotions came up to the surface without warning. 'I'm sorry. I'm sorry, but there's no point anymore. It's *behind* us now. I accept that shutting you out the first time, when we were still together, is on me. I take full responsibility for that. And everything that happened afterwards, as a result. But there's no point dwelling over that anymore. I don't want to know what your intentions were with that girl, or how you felt when she kissed you … and you kissed her back, or anything else, I just can't, okay? I can't! Please don't say anything. You don't know for how long your words will stay in my head and what I'll make of them. I don't need any more new information. I can't even deal with what I already know. I know, I know it sounds insane, but I can't … live like this. I *have* to move on. I have to. This is going to drive me crazy. I can't think about this any longer—'

'Okay, okay,' you said, reaching out for my hand to physically quiet me. 'I get it. We don't have to talk about it. I won't say anything. I've put you through enough.'

I gripped the hand you offered, and we stayed like that for a minute. There was no need to speak anymore. It was done. All of this was behind us. We each had to find some semblance of closure and move on from this. Probably with significant baggage and trust issues, but hopefully manageable.

We sat quietly, thinking about the same thing, holding each other's hand, mourning the loss of our love. It's so unfair that we have to go on living our lives without each other. We had a plan… We had dreams for the future. Everything we had imagined included the other person. But now we had to bury all of that, and move on. Our paths are different now. Our time together is truly over.

I know you were thinking about these things too, but I'm glad you didn't say anything. Instead, we talked about how bad things were at home, how everyone kept freaking out about us and our future and what we've done to bring shame to our respective families. And even though things are still pretty bad at home, there's still so much tension floating around, we managed to find humour in it and laughed together. That laughter we shared was a good distraction from the pain I was feeling in the pit of my stomach.

In that moment, sitting across from you in that coffee shop, I yearned to go back to where we came from. Reverse the clock, be blissfully happy again, even though we are too far gone...

Anyway, there's no point thinking about that now. I'm glad we met today, and no matter how hard it was for me to talk about it, I'm glad it gave you some answers. I'm not sure if it helped you, or if it's going to make things easier or harder, but I am sure we're going to get past this. I'm proud of us for handling this situation like adults. Maybe not fully grown adults, but there's some visible emotional growth for sure.

Tonight, as I'm about to go to bed, I wonder if things will be different tomorrow morning, now that we've talked about it. I hope they are. After a long time, I feel hopeful that we will be okay. We won't be together, but in our separate lives, you will be okay, and I will be okay.

May

I thought that was the last letter I would write to you, but here we are again. To be fair though, these are not letters that I'm actually going to send you, which makes me sound crazy for writing them, but I like to think of it more like a therapy session. Writing therapy. That's a thing, right?

We haven't seen or even spoken to each other since that time at the coffee shop. Wow, it's been almost two months. It's already end of May. If I hadn't run away, we would have been engaged almost six months now. Probably shouldn't talk about all that anymore.

So I write to you today to tell you about all these … experiences I've had in the past couple months. More than anything else, I think I'm trying to make sense of it all by putting them on paper in a sequential manner and then … looking for a pattern, or a story of some sort? I like to document things. You know that. And I figure that I probably won't have these experiences again, and I've come up with this theory...

Okay, let me explain – you know how when things happen, we sometimes don't think about them after they happen, and sometimes we do? Sometimes we think about them for a long time. There's this theory that I thought of, and am testing, where to avoid revisiting old incidents and overthinking, or rethinking them in different lights and coming to different conclusions and wonderments (my thoughts tend to spiral) I'm going to write them down as they happened, with minimal perspective, just facts, and leave it at that. Move on from there. If, down the line, I need to remember something, I know it's on paper, available. This way, keeping memories on paper, I won't be keeping them in my head, cluttering it.

I don't know if it would work, but in theory, I think it's pretty bulletproof. I can just leave things in a folder somewhere, physically let go, and move on with my life. I find that most times the reason I don't let go of things is because I want to make sure my experiences educate me, help me grow and keep me from repeating the same mistakes. However, by remembering everything, I end up with so much clutter in my head, all this baggage, it weighs me down and holds me back from living in a more carefree manner.

I am an old soul, don't necessarily want to do fun, carefree things in life, but I would like some kind of mental peace. I need to balance these lessons from the past with openness for new experiences. This is my attempt at that.

So, you know how everyone's on Tinder nowadays? (I know, cliché again, but hear me out.) Praveen and Deepika insisted that I go on some dates. Apparently, I had nothing to lose. The way I saw it, coming out of such a long-term serious relationship, not to mention my only relationship, going out on Tinder dates was hardly going to help anything

… especially since I don't know what I want. I don't want random hook-ups, I don't want a serious relationship, I don't want to just hang out and waste my own and the other person's time and risk one person getting hurt eventually, so by that logic, Tinder did not make sense at all.

Except that, when we made a profile for me and started swiping, it became a source of entertainment. The internet has always been a place filled with weirdos, but now, there's a platform where these weirdos can actually talk to you. It's interesting. I'm not saying all people on Tinder were like that though. I did end up finding a few I liked and had fun conversations with. Granted, half of the time it was Praveen or Deepika texting them for me.

We didn't take it seriously at all. Until someone I liked asked me out, and then all of a sudden, it was real. He was a real person. I could actually, physically go meet him. And once that door opens, it's kind of a slippery slope from there. I'd be lying if I told you I wasn't excited about this date. He seemed like such a sweet guy. He was five years older than me, and had such a genuine, sweet smile in his Tinder photos.

On the night of my first ever Tinder date (or first date at all, because you and I, we just fell into a relationship, without ever dating first) I was nervous and excited. I was supposed to show the right amount of skin, so as to not be seen as a slut or a nun. I wore my navy dress with long sleeves and boat neck, ending right above my knee, with a pair of sneakers. Carefully put together to give off a cool, but also pretty kind of vibe. Don't know if it worked.

When I saw him waiting outside the restaurant, I knew instantly that it wasn't going to work. He was much ... smaller than he seemed in his pictures. A couple inches taller than me, but pretty much the same build. I know, I'm being shallow. I knew that then too, and I made a deal with myself that I would get one drink with him, to give us a chance to have a conversation and then see how we felt. I wasn't going to bail on someone based solely on their physical appearance.

So, I greeted him with a smile, and we went inside to get a drink. Sitting across from me at the table, he didn't look too small. The pleasant smile I liked was there, the corners of his eyes were crinkling. In the flickering of the tiny tealight, he didn't seem so bad at all.

What he did seem was tired. Not even kidding. It was a Sunday evening, and he had driven back from visiting a friend outside of town, so I get that he must've been exhausted. I had thought initially that it was sweet that he wanted to see me that night, as opposed to waiting till the next weekend, but when your date yawns not once, not twice, but five times in the first forty-five minutes of meeting each other, you kinda know he's not your soulmate.

I didn't want to be rude though, so I tried my best. You have to give someone at least an hour, I've been told. Also, I'm talking as if I was the prize here and was doing him a favour by hanging out with him. That's totally not true. Maybe he didn't like me at all and was giving me an hour as a courtesy too.

To fill the awkwardness, I started talking about my job. I told him what I did, and what I wanted to be doing, small

details about my day – all those impersonal facts to make
conversation while still keeping a distance. What really
bothered me, and it shouldn't have, was his condescending
demeanour in his responses. I mean I get that I'm younger
than him, and I've just started my first real job a couple
months ago, but that doesn't mean he can give me
unwarranted/un-asked-for advice. I was talking about not
wanting to hang out with people from work after work, and
how I think it's sometimes a waste of time, and I want there
to be boundaries between personal and professional lives,
and he gave me a lecture about how I should be more open
to change and accepting of the rules of society. Apparently,
my co-workers will think I'm antisocial if I don't go to every
single happy hour with them.

He was teaching me about work-life balance, as if I
couldn't figure it out myself. He hasn't met any of my co-
workers, so it was surprising that he spoke about how I
should behave around them with such unbridled confidence.
As if regardless of what the reality is, he knows the situation
and is qualified to give advice. The way he told me these
things ... it wasn't a conversation. It wasn't his opinion, it
was fact. His perspective was my reality, even though he
knew nothing about me.

After all the yawning and talking about work, when we
finally walked out, he wanted to walk me to the metro, while
buried into his phone screen, admiring how cheap and
convenient Uber Pool is. I told him that I was okay walking by
myself, and it wasn't super late at night, so he shouldn't worry.
I just wanted to leave. He hugged me goodbye, and said it
was a pleasure to meet me. I thought it was nice of him to lie.

All through our date, he treated me as if I was a child. He was bored, tired, even a little annoyed … but these are the things I sensed. Maybe he didn't actually feel that way. And he didn't (or maybe he did but was lying) because he texted me later that night, reiterating that it had been nice to meet me and that he had fun (what?).

I responded to that text, saying *same*. I honestly expected that to be the end of it, because we were both clearly lying. But then he texted me again the following morning, as I was getting dressed for work. I decided to respond when I got to work, because I was rushed that morning. By the time I reached work, he had sent me three more texts. I responded briefly, with a few words, but that unleashed another seven texts from him. That's when I was done. Later that night, he texted again, but I didn't respond.

Now, let's talk about this for a second. I don't like the concept of ghosting, but I also think that it's okay to make a decision not to engage with someone after it becomes clear that there's nothing there after meeting them for the first time. So that was it, I didn't respond, not because I'm a bad person, but because I didn't want to lead him on. Also, maybe I am a bad person. I don't even know anymore. But he got the hint; I wasn't feeling it, and that was the end of it.

After that date, I was much more careful. The idea of going out, meeting someone new, having a conversation, getting to know someone felt nice, but at the same time, I didn't want to accept any dates unless I was absolutely sure I liked him. I was very keen on not wasting anyone's time, which meant raising my standards and giving it some time, a few conversations, before agreeing to meet. That's how I met Deepanshu.

I'm going to give the ending away – at the end of the date, I was wondering if I actually liked him, or if I just wanted his job. Let me explain. Deepanshu is a creative director at a multinational ad agency. He works on these huge campaigns around the world, in collaboration with big NGOs working for women and children in developing countries, including our own. He travels the world, shooting videos, creating world-class dynamic content to engage with people on digital platforms, mainly social media. Being the creative director of the digital team … that's a job I'd love to have. I'm at least a decade away from that. He started shooting videos when he was sixteen, and in the eleven years since, he's done amazing work on mind-blowing campaigns.

We talked for hours, but in all the time we spent together, I realized later that he talked about himself a *lot*. He was very proud of his achievements (there's nothing wrong with that) and I was asking him all these questions about his work, so it made sense that we were talking about him so much. But clearly, I was just attracted to his job and wanted to be where he was.

All I get to do at my job is what my manager tells me. Create content for social media, marketing emails and sometimes some print – posters, banners, flyers, etc. I don't get to come up with ideas. I thought working for an NGO was going to bring me fulfilment and I would be making a difference and yes, at the end of the day, these projects are shared with the world, and I do find joy in that. But imagine,

conceiving my own ideas, building campaigns ... I'm just
starting, and I have to be patient and learn before I can take
on that kind of responsibility, and also obviously I need to
develop skills to be able to execute these ideas I imagine, but
just thinking about it makes me want it so badly.

Anyway, back to Deepanshu – I showed him some of the
visual content I have created for my company, and he said
that he was impressed and that I was talented. He could've
been lying, but I still appreciated it. At the end of the date,
I realized that we both didn't *feel* anything for each other.
We could hang out more, and could maybe end up liking
each other, but we definitely didn't feel anything that night.

He texted me the following week about something we
talked about, and I responded nonchalantly, but that was
the end of it. Neither of us tried to see each other again.

And that brings us to Dhruv. Him, I really liked. I
remember actually feeling excited when I first matched
with him. Our conversations were happy. He was funny
and I could tell that he was trying to make me laugh. Dhruv
did everything right. He texted first, remembered what
we had talked about before, tried to find things we had in
common and include them in conversations ... little things
like that. He took an actual interest in me, and seemed to
really like me.

The first time we met, I liked him instantly. He was
so calm and collected, happy with where he was in life.
He worked in finance, and I tried not to judge him for
that, because I have close friends who work for banks
and they're wonderful people. Except that my friends

who work in finance have a personality outside of work. Dhruv worked long hours, but when he wasn't working, he had chunks of time where he didn't know what to do with himself. He didn't read books, or have any kind of artistic inclinations or hobbies. He seemed to fill his free time with people and food and alcohol. Which is okay. If that's what makes him happy, I'm no one to judge. It's enough for most people.

Because I've just started working, and there's so much more that I want to learn and do, this whole drinking-eating-socializing thing feels like a waste of time to me. When I come home from work, in the few hours that I have to myself after having dinner and relaxing a little, I want to watch YouTube tutorials about camera tricks and tips, read books about design and content creation, explore online courses I can take, look at what companies that are doing it right are doing with their social media.

I don't want to sit at a bar, talking about things that don't matter. I feel like an old lady when I say this, but it does feel like a huge waste of time. There's so much to learn and do. I don't blame him if he just wants to kick back and relax in his free time. He's done well for himself, probably makes a lot of money, maybe that's what makes him happy. I wish I could find that kind of happiness or fulfilment from my job. I want to be better at everything I do, learn more, create better content, make more of a difference. I want to fill my time with doing things that would get me closer to that. I'm on a journey. He's reached his destination. So, while he's relaxed and happy, I am agitated and nervous.

I know it sounds like a crazy reason to stop seeing someone. We could get used to each other's way of life and maybe meet somewhere halfway. Maybe we could've both been happy, but (here's another one of my theories) I think that it's one thing to try to reason with yourself, and compromise to make it work with someone you love and want in your life. However, if you're finding that you're making excuses for someone from the very beginning, maybe they're not right for you.

I'm all for going to great distances to make it work, to save something that's important to you, but first it has to prove itself. It has to earn the right to your sacrifice.

It should be easy in the beginning. It should be great, it should be the best thing that ever happened to you. It should be something worth fighting for. And whatever I had with Dhruv just wasn't. And once again, I didn't *feel* anything for him. This time though, unlike Deepanshu, Dhruv did really like me.

I tried to tell myself that this could be good for me. This could be what I needed. Someone who's content, comfortable in own skin, satisfied with where he is in life and where he's going. It could be a balancing act, since I am the opposite of that right now.

But that's the difference between checklist and chemistry… Here I present to you another one of my theories: I believe that unless there's something broken (irreversibly), you can make it work with anyone, as long as you believe that the other person is a good person.

Once you get to know each other, you kind of organically meet halfway on things, learn to coexist, which could've happened with me and Dhruv. And if I had a checklist of things I want in the man I date, he would fare pretty well on it. Centred, sensible, attractive, humorous, driven ... he's all of that. But I'm not looking to check boxes off my list, I'm not interested in an arrangement. I'm looking for chemistry. And there was none.

That instant connection, the desire to be with each other without any logical reasoning behind that desire. I want to lose control. I want it to not make sense. I want to be not be able to control my feelings, to be frustrated because my heart refuses to listen to my head. With Dhruv, I was completely in control. We could've made this arrangement work, maybe we could've been happy, but as the cliché goes, there was no passion.

And that's the end of my Tinder chapter. After the first week of knowing Dhruv, when he wanted to hang out more, I already knew by then that we weren't right for each other. I told him the truth, that I thought he was a good human and I enjoyed his company, but I didn't feel a romantic connection, so we shouldn't continue seeing each other. He was very kind in his response. He told me that he respected my honesty, a lot. And that he thought I was an amazing person, and he hoped I would make a difference in the world one day (I had told him about my struggles at work), and wished me luck. We walked away from that experience without any hard feelings. No one got hurt, and I consider that a win.

So there. Three Tinder experiences, all fairly normal (I've heard horror stories) and my lesson at the end of it – I'm not ready to date. I don't have the time or energy to go out and look for a connection. And there's no rush. Also (I probably shouldn't say this, but oh well) it'll be very hard to find someone as amazing as you. What *we* had ... talk about chemistry and passion.

I try not to think about it, but sometimes my thoughts get away from me. I remember how we were with each other. It was as if we were custom designed to work together. We were a team. You had everything I needed, and vice versa. Together, we had everything we could ever need. Like they say in cheesy movies, we completed each other.

Some mornings, I wake up and it takes me a second to remember that you're not here anymore. (I know, I know, my fault.) And I wish I could just go back to sleep and things could go back to *normal*. Before I broke off our engagement, or even before that, when that night with Anamika happened...

But then I remind myself why we are where we are. We could never work. There's a reason why it has to be this way. It's heartbreaking, every time I think of you, but this is the reality we have to live in, and I have come to accept that. Just sometimes...

These checklists and arrangements sound so stupid compared to the intensity of what we shared. I'm in no rush to replace that.

June

ABHAY: Hey. Are you there?

NIDHI: Hi!

ABHAY: What are you up to?

NIDHI: Working on some templates for an Instagram campaign we're launching

ABHAY: Oh, very cool. Excited?

NIDHI: Yes … I mean, mostly

ABHAY: Uh-oh

NIDHI: I know. It's not that serious. Just little problems with some people at work

ABHAY: Wanna tell me about it?

NIDHI: Do you really wanna hear it? Is that what you want to do with your time at 11.29 p.m. on a weeknight?

ABHAY: Can't wait!

NIDHI: Haha, well okay, so I work really hard, and I try to make sure that I never lose drive, I always try to keep a student mentality and be better at everything I'm doing for this company, but even after giving this job everything I have, I sometimes feel so fucking underappreciated at work

63

ABHAY: By your boss?

NIDHI: No. My boss loves my work. She always praises everything I do, and gives me hard projects to work on. I love that. I've only been here a few months and they're already trusting me with bigger projects. It feels great

ABHAY: Then who are these people making you feel underappreciated?

NIDHI: Just bitches at work

ABHAY: Whoa!

NIDHI: No, seriously. People in customer service and office admins, they think that their job is so much more important than mine. Because I spend most of my time either with a camera, shooting around the city, or when I'm in the office, I'm mostly working on designs on Illustrator, or editing videos, or posting on social media — apparently, digital marketing isn't a real job

ABHAY: Are you serious? This coming from people in customer service?

NIDHI: I'm serious. I'm tired of the snide remarks about how easy I have it, and how my work doesn't matter. Like yes, I get it, your work involves day-to-day operations. If something is broken, you get it fixed. If you don't, it remains broken, which is not good. I get that. It's more immediate, with more of a sense of urgency. And my job is more about looking at the big picture, thinking about ways we want people to look at us, expanding our demographic and reach, building audiences and giving them good content. Our day-to-day operations won't stop if I didn't work, but considering that it's not a very big company, and I'm the only person handling digital marketing, I'd say my job is important

ABHAY: Hey, even if you had a team of people working together and you were one of them, your job would still be more important. Their jobs will be taken over by robots eventually. We would be able to feed preprogrammed problems and ways to resolve those problems and with a click of a button, things will work again. They are just part of the machinery, they can be replaced

NIDHI: Wow. That's mean!

ABHAY: Haha! Well, it's the truth. If no one does your job, no one knows about the company, the company doesn't grow and slowly fades into oblivion. Your job requires a brain, and ideas, real skills. Not just a fact sheet. You don't have to read from a manual and match answers to customers' questions all day. You get to do cool shit all day. Making things, and also making a real difference. They're just jealous

NIDHI: I appreciate you taking my side, but you don't even know them!

ABHAY: I don't need to know them. I know the type. Also, whose side are YOU on?

NIDHI: Hahaha, you're right. I should just say thank you

ABHAY: You think?

NIDHI: Thank you!

ABHAY: Okay, better

NIDHI: I'm sorry for piling all of this on you. I've just been really frustrated. The other day, the bosses were away, at a conference, and this admin girl came to peek at my computer screen and asked me what I was working on. Like, bitch, we're not even in the same department. Our jobs NEVER intersect. Why do you need to know what I'm doing at any given point in time? And last week, I was taking some photos for the website, and this one co-worker was in my frame. He didn't realize that because he was on the phone on a work call, so I asked him very nicely if he could just move a couple steps because he was in my shot, and this girl Tina was like, 'Yes, Tushar, move. Nidhi is doing a photoshoot. It's IMPORTANT' with special emphasis on important. I mean this is literally my job. Can you please back the fuck off? I don't know why they behave like this towards me. I'm always friendly with them. I have never gone to any of their desks and asked them what they're working on. Why is it okay for them to ask me that?

ABHAY: Maybe there's nothing else going on in their lives. Maybe they're just bored. Or dissatisfied with their jobs ... or overworked, and then they see you working on such cool projects, having so much fun. I don't think this is about you ... it's just them

NIDHI: I don't know about that... It feels personal. They're nice to everyone else

ABHAY: Well, okay, then let's say it IS personal. Why does that bother you? Do you like them, or want their approval, or ... what?

NIDHI: I think ... it's because I feel like I really tried. See, in the beginning when I first started working, I was kind of a mess. With everything that had happened with us, and this being my first job, I was all over the place. It was nice to meet new people. They were nice to me and I liked them. But then I started hearing gossip about who said what to whom about me, and I stopped talking to them. Not STOPPED stopped, but I was just friendly, never sharing anything that happened outside of the office. I guess that made me a little standoffish. But then week after week, it was such a weight on my shoulders to keep people at arm's length, always walking on eggshells, measuring my words. So then I decided to fix this. I extended an olive branch. I was more open, and friendly, I was nice to everyone and I thought I was making real progress, but then things keep happening and I realize that this is a futile mission. I can never do anything right

ABHAY: Okay, so you tried, and it didn't work. You tried being friendly, you tried giving them space — nothing works. Sounds like it's time to readjust your expectations and move on. Don't expect them to like you or be nice to you. And don't expect a lot of happiness in your workplace. It's okay. I feel like sometimes we tend to put a lot of pressure on ourselves to make sure every single aspect of our lives is perfect. But that can't always happen. It would be great if you could go to work and be carefree and relaxed, everyone got along with each other. But that's not the reality. You can't control other people's behaviour, and you've already tried hard enough. Time to accept it, try not be bothered by it and move on

NIDHI: Ugh, I hate when you're right about stuff. How did you get to be so wisdom-ous?

ABHAY: My wise-ness comes from never caring what people think. Don't get me wrong, you're definitely a better person because you care so much, but I'm happier because I don't

NIDHI: Truth. But also, easy for you to preach — EVERYONE LIKES YOU

ABHAY: I can't deny that

NIDHI: You better not. You're the boss's son. They have to like you

ABHAY: Also, I'm likable

NIDHI: And I'm not?! MEAN

ABHAY: Hahaha! You said it, I didn't

NIDHI: You insinuated it. Anyway ... how's work for you? Probably not as dramatic as mine?

ABHAY: Yeah, can't complain. We're working on this big project, and I'm sort of buckling under the pressure, but I'm doing an okay job of pretending to be fine/under control. I shouldn't even be talking to you right now

NIDHI: Why?

ABHAY: I should be working. But I'm done for the day. It's after midnight, I'm calling it a day

NIDHI: Hmm... Why are you talking to me?

ABHAY: Oh, right. I saw you online, and have been meaning to call you. Thought it would be less aggressive to text and see first

NIDHI: Call me about what?

ABHAY: Prashant's wedding

NIDHI: Oh, that's next month! I totally forgot about it

ABHAY: That's what happens with destination weddings, I guess. Out of sight, out of mind. It's in a few weeks and there are no preparations happening around. Until we fly to Jaipur and suddenly, BOOM, another world

NIDHI: True. Knowing his family, the wedding is going to be a BIG deal. I don't know if we're prepared for what we're walking into

ABHAY: Hahaha I know I'm not. There's definitely going to be elephants and rifles ... maybe even tanks

NIDHI: Tanks is a bit extreme, but I wouldn't be surprised. They're very Rajput in their ways

ABHAY: Yep. So I was going to ask you how you feel about the wedding. I mean, we both have to go

NIDHI: I know. I thought about it too. We can't not go ... and also, I think we're in a good place, right? It won't be awkward

ABHAY: It will be a little awkward

NIDHI: Why do you say that? I mean, yes, the history, but I thought we were okay

ABHAY: We are, but it's a wedding ... and also, I don't know how to say this, so I'm just going to say it. I'm seeing someone. It's only been a month, but we like each other, and I wanted to ask her to come with me. But only if that's okay with you

NIDHI: If I said it's not okay with me, would you not bring her?

ABHAY: If it's honestly not okay with you, yes, I won't bring her. I wouldn't like to put you, her or myself in that situation

NIDHI: That's very sweet of you. But yes, it's okay with me. It's been six months

ABHAY: It has

NIDHI: We knew that we would move on with someone else

ABHAY: Yes, but that doesn't mean that you have to be 100% comfortable with that. It can be awkward at first. And I think that's okay. It's natural, expected. As long as no one gets hurt

NIDHI: No one will. I'll be on my best behaviour

ABHAY: I don't doubt it :)

NIDHI: So, tell me about her. Where did you meet her?

ABHAY: Are we really doing this?

NIDHI: You're right. That's probably taking it too far. Although, if you're happy, I'm happy for you

ABHAY: I know, I appreciate that

NIDHI: It was good to see you the other day. I have mixed feelings about everything we talked about. Not sure if it helped you... But it was an important conversation and I'm glad we got it out of the way

ABHAY: I think so too. It did help, for sure. It's easier to try to move on when you have reasons to, and you know what is happening and why. Talking to you did give me some clarity. And made me stop playing such a victim and take responsibility for my role in it

NIDHI: I don't hold you responsible. It just wasn't meant to be, I guess. I'm glad that it's behind us

ABHAY: Me too. It's definitely getting easier

NIDHI: Yep. The awkwardness has also definitely lowered significantly, which I'm glad about. It feels as though we're slowly reversing the damage ... or maybe moving past it and building something new. A kind of friendship, where it's easy. There's history that makes it complicated, but we're still being adults about it, and I'm proud of us for that

ABHAY: Look at us, being adults

NIDHI: When you first texted me tonight, I didn't know what to think. It was strange for a second. We hadn't decided to be friends (or to not be friends) and you know how my brain makes decisions for me and I like to follow them, as opposed to letting things happen organically and seeing how I feel. So I wasn't sure why you were texting me or what we would/wouldn't talk about. But I guess curiosity won

ABHAY: Hahah! So you're talking to me just out of curiosity. Nice. Makes me feel special

NIDHI: You know what I mean!

ABHAY: I do. I wondered about it too. But then went for it. It's really hard to explain why. I've thought about this. It sounds so tricky, texting your ex, especially so soon after the breakup. I mean, it has been half a year, but considering how long we were together, it's very little time. Also, we didn't talk at all for the first three months, or face the situation head-on, so it feels like a very short time has passed since we got any *closure* as they call it

NIDHI: Agreed. Then what made you text me anyway?

ABHAY: We had to talk about Prashant's wedding sooner or later. And the last time I saw you, we left things in a good place ... I tried to just trust that we'd be okay being adults about this and deal with the situation

NIDHI: Oh, so much faith in us. Adulting has proven to be hard so far, but I feel like we're doing a better job at it now

ABHAY: I agree. And I'm glad too ... about where we are now. This is ... not that hard. When you first left, I didn't think I would ever be able to have an actual conversation with you again

NIDHI: I know what you mean

ABHAY: Especially one where we can talk about things like we used to, with the same comfort level and familiarity ... but without all the pain

NIDHI: I know. I felt the same way. Telling you my work woes was a good idea then? Breaking the ice?

ABHAY: Haha! Yep. Effortless. Nicely done

NIDHI: You're welcome

ABHAY: No, really. It's so you to care so much, and try, and also at the same time be totally frustrated and slightly exaggerate things. But also at the same time, when I take your side and talk shit about them, you have to run and take their side and defend them

NIDHI: They're not here to defend themselves! It's unfair!

ABHAY: You're ridiculous

NIDHI: You already knew that

ABHAY: Yep. It was nice to rediscover that tonight though

NIDHI: It was nice to have you on my side (before I switched sides)

ABHAY: I wasn't surprised

NIDHI: I really wish things were better at work, but you're right. It's okay if things are not perfect in all spheres of my life, all the time. So I'm gonna try to live with it. Thanks for your wise-ness

ABHAY: You're welcome. Being so wisdom-ous is a privilege and a responsibility

NIDHI: Okay, now you're making less and less sense. Time for bed

ABHAY: Time for bed. I was slightly worried about how this conversation about the wedding would go. But thank you for making this easy

NIDHI: Of course! I'd hate to make it difficult. I've made many things difficult enough already

ABHAY: No, please. Both of us, we need to stop trying to place blame on ourselves. Past. We established that. Let's move forward...?

NIDHI: Let's.

ABHAY: Good. Same page. Glad

NIDHI: Your wise-ness is showing again

ABHAY: Hahaha. It's a curse

NIDHI: Apart from being a privilege and responsibility? That's a lot

ABHAY: It is. Sometimes my neck hurts (cuz my brain is so big)

NIDHI: That's from a movie

ABHAY: Dammit

NIDHI: Hahaha, okay, we should go zzz now. I'll see you at the wedding, and we'll make it not awkward

ABHAY: Deal

NIDHI: Goodnight!

ABHAY: (Already zzz-ing)

July

Dragging her suitcase behind her, Nidhi walked out of the airport, the glass doors parting for her. She set her handbag on top of her suitcase and pulled out her cell phone. Someone named Sumi was supposed to receive her at the arrivals gate. She mentally prepared herself for awkward small talk and *how do you know the bride/groom* questions. There were going to be a lot of those this weekend.

But of course, that wasn't going to be the hardest or most awkward part of her weekend. No, that would be being around Abhay. *And his new girlfriend.* Nidhi had been taken aback when he'd told her about the new girl, but obviously, she'd behaved as if she didn't care at all. But how couldn't she care? Now that she'd had more time to adjust to the news, a part of her was genuinely happy for him. However, there was no denying that there would be some amount of discomfort and awkwardness between the three of them. But overall, they'd all be able to make it out alive.

She looked around, searching for Sumi. Maybe she should take a cab to the hotel, but then she would have to let Prashant know to coordinate with this Sumi person, who might/might not be waiting for her. Her thumb hovered over the call option on her phone, just as the thought of turning around and going back home flitted through her mind.

'Nidhi!' Prashant called out to her from between the crowd of people assembled to receive their loved ones. Damn it; too late.

Nidhi put on a smile. 'Oh wow! The groom *himself*. I am honoured,' she exclaimed, shuffling towards him, bags in tow.

'Yeah, only the best treatment for my most special guests.' Prashant smiled broadly as he hugged her.

'Guests, plural…?' Nidhi barely had a chance to finish her thought before Prashant yelled excitedly again, a bit too loudly, right in her ear. He released her and opened his arm for his other guests.

'Abhay!' Prashant hugged him and patted his back. After releasing him too, he turned to Abhay's girlfriend and shook her hand. 'And Simran. Welcome, welcome.'

Her name is Simran, Nidhi thought. Ugh, gag. Okay, control yourself. She's probably a lovely person whose parents chose her name under the influence of a DDLJ hangover; she shouldn't be blamed for that. She probably already had been punished with too many 'Simran as in *Raj aur Simran*' jokes in her life. One should refrain from judgement.

'Hi,' Abhay said, and gave her a half hug.

'Hey!' Nidhi returned brightly. She quickly removed herself from his hug and turned to Simran. 'Hi Simran!'

'Hey! Nidhi, right?' Simran smiled, looking a little nervous.

Nidhi softened. This couldn't be easy for anyone, but she was going to try her best to make sure she didn't add to the already complicated situation in a negative way. 'Yes, it's so nice to meet you.' She smiled back.

They hugged each other and then, after a very brief awkward pause, everyone grabbed their bags and walked towards the car. Nidhi took controlled breaths. She could smell Abhay, and feel Simran on her side, as they walked. So far, so good. *Just put one step in front of the other, and before you know it, this will be behind you.*

*

The first day wasn't proving to be too bad. Some might call it fun, even. She hadn't expected it to be. Lately, she'd been finding herself being very glass-half-empty about situations. Her scepticism for this situation was valid – sharing a roof with her ex-boyfriend and his new girlfriend for an entire weekend for a wedding, when she had left the aforementioned ex-boyfriend at their engagement party … that can't be fun for anyone. However, once the festivities began, she had to admit that she had been freaking out more than she had needed to.

They were shown to their rooms as soon as they arrived at the resort, where there were elaborate cold beverages waiting for them. She had been counting on the cocktails to make it through the weekend. Everything happened very fast. Once she showered and changed, she was ushered to a backyard garden, where there was loud music blaring from the speakers and a selection of food and drinks spread out on a long table against the wall.

The backyard was filled with people, dressed in bright colours and shiny jewellery.

Nidhi hesitated, but only for a second, before joining everyone else in the celebration. She was genuinely excited to see all her friends from college, some of whom she hadn't been in touch with for longer than she liked. Once she found her people, there was laughter, drinking and dancing for hours. Not to mention so. much. food.

But even while she was dancing to upbeat Bollywood remixes with her old friends, part of her was always on alert. Without realizing it herself, she kept an eye on the door at all times. Eventually, Abhay did come out with Simran and Nidhi's heart took a violent lunge. All of her energy for the next few songs was focused on keeping her expression as neutral as possible. She couldn't ignore them, but also couldn't overcompensate by being too friendly. She had to find a balance, tailor her behaviour to show she was totally cool with everything.

It soon turned out that she had once again been overthinking it. Because once the new couple joined them on the dance floor, there was barely any awkwardness. Nidhi met Abhay's eyes and he smiled at her, making funny dance moves, which made her laugh and relax a little. She met Simran's eyes, who took it as an invitation. Simran danced over to Nidhi, held both her hands and lifted them up, moving back and forth with the music. Nidhi wasn't sure how she felt about dancing with Simran, but played along. *Be cool, be cool, be cool.*

After a few songs, everyone was visibly more relaxed. Abhay seemed happy. Simran seemed nice. Nidhi was okay.

Dancing with her old friends, a little under the influence of booze and great food, and the overall cheerful energy, Nidhi ... unclenched. She let go of all the tension she'd been carrying on her shoulders for what had seemed like forever, and let herself enjoy the present. It felt good.

✳

By the time it was the big day, Nidhi couldn't believe how smoothly everything had gone and how much fun she had had. Some of them had taken short road trips to visit the local markets and old palaces. She was in good company, surrounded by people with positive energy. Everyone seemed to be using the time to get away from the rush of their everyday life and kick back, without a worry in the world.

It was contagious. She absorbed that energy and relaxed too. When the day of the wedding arrived, she looked back at her weekend and marvelled at how smoothly it had gone so far.

'Time really flies, huh?' she said, as she carefully divided the pallu of her saree into measured pleats, getting dressed for the wedding.

'I know, right? I feel like I just got here,' Jyoti said. Jyoti was one of Nidhi's closest friends from college, who had moved away for a job after graduation. Which meant that they didn't see each other very often anymore. However, whenever they did see each other, they went back to how things were, as if no time had passed in between at all. They didn't have to do a whole lot to maintain their friendship. They simply ... were friends. No amount of distance or time changed that. Nidhi still felt comfortable talking to Jyoti about anything and everything.

'Yep. I'll return home all fat and sleepy,' Nidhi said. 'But no complaints.'

'Those aren't the worst things to be. At least you're happy...?'

Nidhi felt Jyoti watching her carefully. She knew where this was going, and didn't necessarily want to launch into a conversation about Abhay, so she tried to brush it off by laughing. 'Happier than I'd expected, for sure.'

'Were you so super nervous about how things would go with ... you know who?'

'You can say his name. I'm not going to break down at the mention of my ex-boyfriend's name. And besides, that was a long time ago. We've all moved on with our lives.'

'That's right, you're right,' Jyoti said quickly, backtracking. 'I'm glad there aren't any bad feelings between you guys.'

'You and me both,' Nidhi said. She turned to show Jyoti her saree. 'How does this look?'

'Not bad. Let me just fix this...' Jyoti attacked portions of Nidhi's saree, while Nidhi watched their reflection in the mirror.

'You know what, I'm actually really proud of both Abhay and myself for being such adults about this. We could've so easily let this be a messy, bitter experience for the both of us, but we somehow managed to have fun. We've actually even managed to kinda sorta develop a new kind of friendship with each other. There's familiarity there, and so many memories, which can be painful, but it feels like we're just keeping the good and ignoring the bad,' Nidhi said.

'I know what you mean. It shows. You guys are handling this way better than any of us could've expected. Unless it's all pretence...' Jyoti said. She stood up and twirled Nidhi around, admiring her work on the saree. 'Perfect. So, is it?'

'What is what?'

'Is it all pretence? Are you both just pretending to be okay?'

'What?! Don't be ridiculous,' Nidhi protested.

'Nidhi.' Jyoti gave her a look. She was never too pushy, but she always knew how to get her friend to talk.

'Okay, fine,' Nidhi said, gritting her teeth. 'Maybe there is *some* discomfort there. Some, not a lot. And that's expected, right? We're only human. We can't erase years and years of memories and pretend as if nothing happened, and we're all just completely fine. Are there some cracks in our perfect demeanour? Yes. But are we just pretending to be fine while we're truly miserable inside and pining for each other? Definitely no.'

'I never said that you were secretly pining for each other. Just that ... it was a long, intense relationship. We all thought you guys were going to be together forever. You can't move on from that unscathed.'

'Well, there's *some* scathing. But it's manageable.'

'As long as it's manageable,' Jyoti said and took one last look around the room. 'You have the keys?'

'Yes.' Nidhi patted her clutch.

'Time for the big night. Ready to do this?'

'Let's do it.'

They left the room together. As Nidhi turned around to check the lock on the door, Jyoti said, 'Manageable is okay … but only if it's getting better every day.' She pulled Nidhi into an unexpected hug, bringing tears to both their eyes, before they rushed to the wedding upstairs.

*

The bride was beautiful, the groom's smile couldn't have been wider, the atmosphere was lit with cheer and romantic music, the smell of roses wafting across the lavishly decorated terrace. Yellow, twinkling string lights brought a fairy-tale-like feel to the roof. Yellow and white roses were tied together in long strings that looped around the pillars of the mandap. The rooftop itself was gigantic, so the guests were spread out and relaxed.

Nidhi tried not to think about what her wedding would've looked like if she hadn't run away from her engagement. The wedding would've been later this year. Her parents had wanted to reserve a hotel for the venue, but Abhay and she had wanted to have the ceremony outdoors. She looked around at the beautiful setting around her, and even standing in the open air, she had trouble breathing.

The back of her throat choked up, and she gulped hard. *It's alright, it's alright, it's alright*, she repeated to herself like a mantra. *I made this decision, it's the right choice, we've both moved on, we're in a good place, this is just a momentary crisis that shall pass, everything's going to be fine. Just smile; Jyoti was right, as long as it's manageable and getting better every day, that's progress. It's alright, it's alright, it's alright.* She sighed loudly and tried to shake herself out of her own head.

When she turned around, the first thing she saw was Abhay walking out to the roof. It didn't help her breathing. He was wearing a faded burgundy sherwani that stretched comfortably across his wide chest. It was like a scene from a cheesy movie. He walked casually, almost carelessly, in his Punjabi jootis, his hair slicked to the side, coming out the door, looking around for a familiar face.

Before Nidhi could form another thought, he spotted her and waved. She waved back. As he strolled towards her, her heart began to pound loudly in her chest. *It's just the atmosphere,* she told herself sternly, just as a question popped up in the back of her mind. *What is happening to me, what is happening to me, what is happening to me…?*

'You look amazing!' he said when he got within her earshot.

How did he do that? So nonchalantly, as a greeting … how come he was so relaxed and comfortable around her, when she could feel sweat beads appear on her forehead any second? This was not fair. She tried to copy what he did and returned cheerfully, 'Look who's talking!'

'Aw, stop. You're just lying to me to protect my feelings!'

'You caught me. Oops!' Nidhi teased. They laughed, and as if feeling guilty about that laugh, she immediately enquired, 'Where's Simran?'

'She was taking forever to get dressed. Some disaster with ... something. They have a team down there with safety pins of all shapes and sizes to control the damage,' Abhay explained.

The way he was looking at her made her look everywhere else. She found herself unable to meet his eyes. She tried to cover her awkwardness by saying, 'It's a hard life, man. Took me forty-five minutes to get into this. I mean, maybe putting it on only took five minutes, but there was a lot of adjusting and readjusting, a lot of safety pins to safely pin everything in place and make it perfect.'

'Looks like it worked.' His eyes travelled down her body, admiring her saree. Before he jerked his head and turned away, as if realizing what he'd been doing, Nidhi saw something in his eyes. It looked very similar to how she felt inside. *He wanted her. He still wanted her.*

She could be wrong ... but she'd known him for far too long, and seen that look in his eyes far too many times, to be this mistaken. He wanted her. He may never act on it, it may be a momentary thing which will pass within seconds, or eventually, but right then, in that moment, she knew that he wanted her.

The knowledge calmed her. It wasn't just her. She wasn't crazy. This wasn't unusual. It was okay to feel things. They were in very close proximity after a long time, and the last time they had been this close, they were in love, anticipating a life together. It was okay to still feel fragments of those emotions every once in a while. Not everything in life can be controlled just by your brain sending a signal and the heart following the instructions. Sometimes the heart takes over, and that's okay.

'Uh, thanks,' she said meekly.

Abhay cleared his throat.

They were quiet, both thinking about the same thing, but not accepting it, especially not to each other. Nidhi still believed that if she supressed certain things long enough, they went away. She hoped this was one of them, even as the cool breeze brought a fresh waft of scent to her nostrils. His scent. Her breathing got troubled, her palms clammy. She clenched her fists into balls, to stop herself from reaching out and moving that one strand of hair away from his forehead. It felt so natural ... it would be so easy to go back to being with each other.

In that moment, without sharing a word, or even a look, just by standing next to each other, close, but too far away, Nidhi had trouble remembering any of the reasons why they couldn't be together.

'There you are!' Simran called from behind them, and both Abhay and Nidhi spun around, as if physically shaken out from another world.

'There you are!' Abhay repeated brightly, holding out his hand for Simran. 'I see that the damage has been controlled.'

'Yes!' Simran said, looking from Abhay to Nidhi and back at Abhay, her brows giving away her confusion/displeasure at finding them with each other. Her tone wasn't as friendly this time when she said, 'Hey, Nidhi. Love your saree.'

'Thanks,' Nidhi said, smiling. 'You look beautiful.'

After a few minutes of essential small talk, where she was proud of herself to have been extremely pleasant and not at all uncomfortable, at least to the untrained eye, she excused herself to go congratulate the happy couple. She walked away from Abhay and Simran, putting one foot in front of the other, deliberately counting her steps.

As long as it's manageable. As long as it gets better every day.

*

With her luck, Nidhi wasn't surprised to find herself taking the same flight as Abhay and Simran. They decided to split a cab to the airport, because not doing that would be suspicious, as if something was wrong. And even though something was wrong, life is all about keeping up pretences, isn't it? *I'm fine, he's fine, everyone is fine.*

Everyone was not fine. Simran clearly wasn't. If not for Simran's behaviour towards Nidhi ever since she found Abhay standing next to her in the middle of the rooftop bustling with wedding guests, Nidhi could've tried to forget about the strange moment between her and Abhay the previous night.

Simran had been visibly cold towards Nidhi. So Nidhi's brief moment of … nothing with Abhay was not what preoccupied her mind as they made their way to the airport. She took the front seat, so Abhay and Simran could sit together in the back. Nidhi thought she was putting on a good show, but Simran had clearly sensed something. Abhay was also behaving strangely. He was either uncomfortable or angry.

Had Abhay and Simran talked about Nidhi? What was there to talk about? Did Simran bring up the moment from the previous night? How did they talk about her behind her back? Was she the villain in their story? Did they hate her?

Nidhi felt like her head was about to explode. Once they reached the airport, she excused herself to go to the ladies' room and from then onward, they went their separate ways. They smiled at each other while boarding the flight, and half hugged after landing. Nidhi found a cab and let herself be driven in the opposite direction of where Abhay and Simran were headed.

August

4 August

I'm still thinking about it … the moment on the rooftop, and Simran's behaviour towards me following that. Abhay, I can't stop wondering how Simran and you talk about me when I'm not there. Do you tell her things about me? About us? How we used to be, what we did, moments we spent together, things we talked about? I'm assuming she doesn't want to talk about me a whole lot, does she? *I* wouldn't want to know too much about my boyfriend's relationship with his ex.

I've tried not to think about it, or let it affect me, but I can't get it out of my mind. I haven't been very good at letting things go recently, have I? Regardless of what I tell myself, I clearly haven't moved on. I really, really wanted to move on from our breakup and start over. I thought I was making progress too, but now, all of a sudden, I feel myself slipping backwards.

I'm so frustrated with myself. I've disappointed myself so many times, I've lost count. It's just what I do now. I have circular thoughts, they loop around in my head, I feel them coiling around my throat, anxiety slithering like snakes in the pit of my stomach.

Well, at least I don't feel like that all the time. It comes and goes. When it's away, I can be normal, do normal things, play my character in this world. Then it comes back, and I feel the same shock as I did the first time. I wish I could say it gets better every day, but that would just be a white lie. It doesn't get better. It doesn't necessarily get worse either. It's kind of just … there. It exists, just like I do.

Anyway, it's here now, so I wanted to address it and move on (possibly). Not sure if I'll move on (work in progress), but I'll address it here, there's no harm in that. These letters have been helpful so far. I'll stop writing soon, I promise, because I do realize that this is kinda crazy, writing in this vacuum, to no one. But life is kinda crazy right now too. So it makes sense if you think about it.

If she does talk about me, why should it bother me? It really shouldn't, but I still wonder. That day in the cab ride to the airport, I had a distinct feeling that the two of you had had a conversation … maybe even an argument involving me. I apologize if I caused problems between you guys. My sole intention while going on this trip was to make the weekend as pleasant as possible for everyone involved.

Did she ask you what you and I were talking about when she joined us on the terrace? Was she angry with you for being with me? What did you say? That it was nothing, you were just being friendly, and it meant nothing?

I'm not sure I'm prepared for your answer to that.

I keep reminding myself that this isn't about Simran. None of this is about her, and I shouldn't have any kind of feelings towards her, especially negative. She came to your life *after* us. There's no overlap, none of this involves her, none of the blame goes to her. Whatever she thinks of me, whatever role I play in her life … it shouldn't matter to me. It's her life, her prerogative.

But sometimes, I can't help but wonder if she does talk about me, how you respond. I wonder how you talk about me behind my back. Am I evil, or heartless, or just a loser? Guys like to call their exes crazy. That one's everywhere – you ask a dude why his relationship ended, and he would tell you, *oh, that girl was crazy*. That's apparently a valid reason. Do you guys think I'm crazy?

Most of all, I wonder if the words you say about me to her reflect your true feelings.

*

9 August

This past week has been so … disjointed. I can't seem to find the simplest words in the simplest conversations, I can't be productive at work because my mind keeps drifting off to a whole another world, I'm unable to do the easiest of tasks, my body just doesn't cooperate with the broken signals my brain sends it.

I feel lightheaded *all the time* and no matter what I do, I'm always tired and sort of just walking around in a daze. Yesterday, Maa, concerned about me, felt my forehead to discover that I was a little warm. It's a very mild fever, but now I have to stay home for a few days as a precaution. Maa refuses to let me go out and live my life till my temperature returns to normal, and my eyes look less ghost-like.

Honestly, at this point, I'm relieved to have a valid excuse to take a few days off and not do life.

Not gonna lie, staying home and being taken care of feels good. Things are finally getting back to normal at home. Or maybe everyone is just putting their anger/disappointment on hold till I stop looking like someone on their deathbed. I'm exaggerating. Apologies. It's really not that bad.

Also, if I'm being honest with you (and still exaggerating) I actually like the fever. It has a strange cleansing effect. It feels good to burn.

On a less dramatic note, in all this free time I have now, just lying in bed all day, I began thinking about where I want my career to go. Which resulted in me starting a brand-new job search. I like mine, yes. It's interesting, keeps me occupied and stimulated, provides meaning to my otherwise primarily boring existence. But I really could be doing more.

I'm okay, but I'm not happy. I can't blame my job for all of it, but if I can fix this, I can lighten the sadness load a little. I've decided to consciously make a change in my life to find more happiness. One day at a time. With my job, I believe that if at the end of every day, I feel that I've been productive, it would be fulfilling. Fulfilment will bring happiness. At least that is my hope.

I don't have control over all aspects of my life, but I can control this. I have been unsure about my career path for the longest time, ever since we graduated college, actually. When I chose this job, it was a thought-out, deliberate decision. I don't think it was a bad one, but it also isn't the perfect fit. I could be doing more. I don't know what … but I could be doing more.

Look at me making plans again. When I don't have plans, everything's in free-fall and that freaks me out. I make plans and then things don't go my way, again – I freak out. There's no winning here, but I'm trying!

I envy you for your certainty. The ease with which you found your place in your family business and the drive with which you have been working ever since, it's commendable. You first began doing it because your family needed you to. Even though it wasn't your passion, you stepped up to the responsibility. But it turned out to be a blessing in disguise. You found something you love to do, and haven't looked back.

I, on the other hand, have been imagining all these different lives I could be living if I choose one path or the other, and am unable to find something … to keep.

I'm working on it.

*

16 August

Happy birthday, Abhay.

I am a person with obsessive tendencies, as we're aware. So, like everything else, this too was a point of much consideration. I wondered if I should call you, or send you a text. A month ago, I probably would've just called you, pretended we were cool, and that would've been the end of it.

But now … I don't know what's appropriate anymore. Weren't things better before that night at Prashant's wedding? We were both okay (mostly) and moving on (at least on the surface) and overall in an okay place. But ever since that night, I've been having these feelings ... and I can't tell if they're just residual emotions from before, when we were in love, or if I'm developing feelings for you again. That would be bad.

In that moment, on the rooftop, did you feel what I felt too? You can tell me you didn't. I won't believe you. I was there, I saw the look in your eyes. It was fleeting, only there for a second, but I know what I saw.

Ever since coming back from Jaipur, I have been thinking more and more about you. I sometimes wonder if you think about me too. I won't ask, and you shouldn't tell me, because I'm not prepared for either of the two answers.

If you do think about me, I won't know what to do with myself.

And if you don't think about me, well, that information might just kill me.

I'm not doing so good, Abhay. I can't stop thinking about you; the physical and emotional distance feels like a rope closing around my throat. I know you blame yourself and I blame myself, and we both probably blame each other too ... but at this point, it doesn't matter whose fault it was.

Not to me, not anymore. Finding a person or an incident to blame doesn't help, at all. It doesn't change the reality, which is that we ended and you have moved on. To a third person, it may seem like I have too. I have so much going for me. I have close friends who love me, I have a great first job working on amazing projects, my family is finally letting me be family again, I've been on dates with very nice people (if that's important) – life doesn't appear so bad.

However, the reality of the situation is that this ... checklist doesn't make me happy. I appreciate all of these things, yes. I understand that it may be more than what most people can hope for, which makes me feel ungrateful, but I can't shake this feeling that I am living in someone else's skin. I'm playing a character, living someone else's life. It's a very unsettling sensation.

Abhay, my life feels empty. I go days and weeks just living like a robot, doing all these things we are supposed to do, but then one day I stop, and I ask myself what I'm doing anything for. Nothing makes me happy. I think I have just become a miserable person. I truly, deep in my heart, have begun to believe that I will never be happy again.

The thought of you not being in my life anymore ... it shatters me. Even now, eight months after *I* ended things, I still feel as broken as I did on day 1. When it happened in the beginning, I would simply repeat to myself why I did what I did. I would tell myself that we would never have gotten over our problems, we would never have been happy together, that it made total sense to move on and start over – I *knew* it in my gut. I *had to* leave. We *had to* end things.

Now, when I try to go back and think of all the reasons we couldn't work, I can think of none. I guess that's the thing about feelings. They're fleeting.

When I left you, I *knew* it was the right decision. It was what we needed, it was the right decision for the both of us, the only thing to do. It didn't feel like a choice. But *why*? I struggled with answering that question for months. I didn't know *why* then, I certainly don't know *why* now. That's the problem with following a gut feeling, instead of your brain, or reason. Because these gut feelings can abandon you at any given moment and switch sides.

It's not all negative. After we ended, I did stop worrying about being cheated on or betrayed. The nightmares did stop, I did stop feeling as if I was walking on very thin glass that could shatter at any moment and my entire world could collapse. I stopped wondering where you were, if you were talking to someone. I used to feel threatened by the smallest things. All of that did go away. I no longer had a weight on my shoulders that I carried around with me everywhere I went – questioning everything, always sceptical of anything anyone said… It felt good to live without trust issues, and I focused on that in the beginning.

Being alone does provide me the luxury of not living in a constant state of alertness, expecting my life to turn upside down any minute. So maybe that peace of mind is worth a life without you. It doesn't feel like that right now.

Right now, it feels … impossible. To live without your voice in my ear, your scent in my nose, your touch on my skin, your eyes in my eyes, your taste on my lips.

*

26 August

ABHAY: Hey, how's it going?

NIDHI: Hey. Good. What's up?

ABHAY: I wanted to ask you a quick question. It might be a little strange though

NIDHI: What is it?

ABHAY: Well, I wanted to know if when we were together, did you ever feel as if I wasn't attentive enough, or that I didn't care about what was going on in your life or things you care about?

NIDHI: What are you talking about? Never.

ABHAY: Really? You always felt you were getting everything you wanted or needed from me?

NIDHI: Yes. You were a good boyfriend, Abhay. I mean, we had our problems in the end, but while we were together, you were always good to me. Funny, thoughtful, caring. I don't remember feeling any sort of disappointment.

ABHAY: Hmm

NIDHI: What's going on?

ABHAY: You're probably the last person I should share this with

NIDHI: What do we have to lose? We've lost everything anyway

ABHAY: Don't say that

NIDHI: It's true

ABHAY: Just don't say it, please. Anyway, recently, Simran has not been the happiest girlfriend. And I think it's my fault. She ... the other day, she told me that she thought I was shutting her out, and not being completely honest with her. That just threw me off

NIDHI: Because you feel like you are being open and honest with her?

ABHAY: I think I am. I tell her everything I think I know ... but then there are things that are unresolved, that I don't know the answers to ... I myself don't know how I feel about them, and I can't tell her something that's not true, so by that logic, I'm probably keeping things from her

NIDHI: What kind of things?

ABHAY: I ... really shouldn't. I mean, things like, when she asks how I feel about something, I have to think about it for a second before I respond. Because either 1) I honestly don't know how I feel about it and 2) I have to make sure I don't say something that hurts her feelings

NIDHI: Okay, I don't know what you're talking about here, but if she's asking you something directly, you have to trust that she's ready for your answer. Yes, no, maybe, I don't know — whatever it is, she has probably already thought of all possibilities before asking you, if it's something important

ABHAY: But that doesn't mean she can't be hurt by my response

NIDHI: You're right, yes. But she asked you, so you owe her the truth. You have to show her all the cards, and she's the one who gets to decide what she wants to do with the information. Hiding the truth, whatever it is, is not going to change it. She just won't be in on it, which is probably how she feels, if she's saying you shut her out

ABHAY: You don't know how complicated this is

NIDHI: I guess I don't. But with the little information I've been given, this is my best advice. Honesty over lies, always

ABHAY: That's good advice. I don't know how it helps me though

NIDHI: Give her some credit, Abhay. She's probably not as fragile, or in need of protection, as you think she is. I understand your instinct to try to protect her, it's very sweet. But she doesn't need to be left out while you try to find the answers for yourself. Include her, work on the problems together. I'm sure she would appreciate the openness. She's clearly in love with you. Give her a chance. If you're not honest now, it only gets worse from here. You don't want to build a relationship on a weak foundation

ABHAY: You're making a lot of sense right now

NIDHI: Ha, you've found me on one of my better days. Anyway, I have to go now. Good luck with all this!

September

I hope things are okay with Simran and you. I feel bad for the way we left things after Jaipur. So unnecessary, after everything was going so well. She seems like a sweet, genuine person, and she's clearly in love with you.

You seemed happy too, at least till the night of the wedding. Ever since then, I don't know. I don't know where you are and what you are and aren't thinking. For all I know, you could be exactly where I am, or miles and miles apart. I have no way to tell, and I've been trying not to assume anything.

Let me explain. The other night, when you were asking me all those questions about how I felt about your emotional availability when we were together, I didn't ask you why you needed to know. I can only assume. If she thinks you're closed off and unavailable, then there's certainly something different about your relationship with her. Because when we were together, never, not once did I think that you were shutting me out. I never craved more closeness, and hoped you would give me more.

Yes, I wanted to be with you all the time, and missed you when we weren't together, but I never wondered if you were thinking about me or not. I never wished I could get to know you better. We were happy, comfortable. I knew who you were as a person, the little things and the big ones. I never thought of you as a closed book. I never felt left out, or wondered what was going on in your head.

You felt the same way about me. Our desire to be with each other came from our love for each other, not our need to control. And we didn't *need* to control each other, because we were sure in the fact that in a way, we already had control over the other person. It's called love.

We loved each other like crazy. Everything we did, together or alone, we always knew that we were loved unconditionally. There were no questions or doubts. We knew each other inside-out and loved every bit about the other person. Until…

Anyway, I thought of all of this when you told me how Simran feels. You're not emotionally unavailable, so if she's feeling that you are, it's probably something you did. (Maybe you are emotionally unavailable *to her*). Unless it's some sort of baggage she's carrying from before. But in my experience, I've seen that girls have a sort of intuition about these things. If you're making her feel like this, like she's not enough, or if you can't give her all of you, or all she wants, you probably shouldn't string her along. It's unfair to the both of you, especially to her.

When I say that maybe you're emotionally unavailable to her, I don't mean you're trying to be that way. Maybe you don't even see it. But she does. If she feels that way, maybe it's true. Maybe you should think about what you're doing that's making her feel like that.

Of course, I can say none of this to you. The ex-girlfriend telling you to how to treat your new girlfriend … that's not okay. Besides, this is just me trying to string random pieces together. I could be miles away from reality.

Just like you could've been miles away from where I was that night on the rooftop. I can't get it out of my head. That look in your eyes … it's driving me crazy. But it could've just been me, building parallel realities in my head, while in the literal reality, you felt something for a brief second, possibly out of habit, and moved on in the very next second, never thought about it again.

Or you're exactly where I am. Thinking about it every single night since that night, unable to shake the feeling that we've made a terrible mistake. That we're going down the wrong path. This is not how our story is supposed to end…

But again, all speculations. You could be miles away. None of this matters anyway. We've all moved on, haven't we? I have to stop being the loser who can't stop living in the past. It's getting quite pathetic now. I don't like myself anymore. I can't remember the last time I liked myself, or felt like my existence was adding positive value to the world around me. But I don't want to think about it; that's a rabbit hole I can't get in right now.

Let's change the topic. I have some good news! I got a job interview with this NGO based in Delhi, that works to raise funds to put underprivileged kids back in school. It's a new organization, but with a sensible business model. It being owned by Rajeev Kapoor helps with funding and branding; having a Bollywood A-lister makes everything easier. If I get the job, I would be doing mostly branding – working with the digital marketing team to do research, raise awareness, put the organization on the map.

I'm trying not to get too excited about this job, because I'm not sure they like me there. The day of the interview … was a strange one. I had woken up from a restless sleep. The stress for the interview, teamed with the haphazard research I had done to prepare for it resulted in these … colourful images in my dreams. It was a mixture of pictures I saw in the articles I'd read the night before, the disturbing data, and my own constant state of panic about wasting my life when I could be doing more, something to make a real difference.

By the time I reached their offices – with bags under my eyes, my lips chapped, almost bloody with worry, my palms sweaty – I felt as if the battle was already half lost. I did my best, but instead of taking charge and showing them everything I can do for them, I was more … grappling to find things from my portfolio that best reflected my skills and my default tone was please-hire-me-I'll-do-anything.

Sometimes I feel like I can do anything I set my mind to. Yes, I know that's super cheesy, but if I'm working on something I love and truly believe in, even if I don't have all the skills and experience necessary to finish a job, I can learn. I'm excited to think up innovative marketing ideas, and then do whatever needs to be done to arrive at the result. All I need is for someone to take a chance. Give me a shot and I'll prove myself. I just want them to give me a chance.

I don't think they're going to call me back. But at least from this experience, I now know what *not* to do the next time I go to an interview. I started on the wrong foot, and kept slipping. Next time, I'll prepare more. I've always sucked at interviews.

Do you remember the interview you drove me to, one of the first ones I got, right after graduation? In the car, you kept telling me to calm down, while I aggressively jumped from article to article, trying to find out everything I could about the company and the work they did. I was looking up their competitors and their work, when you finally put your foot down.

'Okay, I have to take this away from you now,' you said, snatching my phone.

I reflexively lunged to get it back, but you wouldn't let me have it. I was exasperated. 'Are you serious right now? I have an interview in twenty-two minutes!'

'Are *you* serious right now?' you repeated without flinching. 'You have an interview in twenty-two minutes.'

'What's your point?'

'You have got to chill. You can't go in there like this.'

'What is *that* supposed to mean?' I asked heatedly, wiping my sweaty palms on my pleated trousers.

You motioned towards all of me, and said, smiling, 'This. You look like a cartoon character. With your knitted eyebrows, pink cheeks and beads of sweat on your forehead. And while I find this funny, people who are meeting you for the first time and are potentially going to pay you money to work for them might not see you as a candidate to invest in.'

'You're saying I'm not good enough!' I yelled.

'What do you think? In all the time that you've known me ... please answer this question for yourself. Do you think I think you're not good enough?'

I glared at you, puffing angrily. After a moment, I muttered, 'The answer better be no.'

'Of course it is! You deserve this, and so much more. I know that, you know that, but they don't. You have to show them. And they won't be able to see the best of you if you present this ... mess to them. No offence, but I wouldn't hire this girl either.'

'My God. Do you have a point here, or are you just trying to kick me when I'm down?'

'I'm not trying to kick you. I'm trying to question why you're down in the first place. You are in the top ten per cent, wherever you go, whatever you do. You'll be amongst the people in the room that are doing it the best. You're organized, you are attentive to details, you think things through, no one can beat your planning and reasoning skills – you have all the raw materials. Your OCD is one of your biggest strengths, when it comes to this job role. The only problem I see here is this crippling lack of confidence that seems to have come out of nowhere and overtaken everything.'

I thought about that for a second. 'First of all, thank you for making fun of my OCD. And it's not unreasonable to be nervous before an interview. I really need this job. I can't mess it up!'

'Do you?' You turned towards me and raised your eyebrow in question.

'Want this job? Yes! Why do you think I'm panicking?!'

'I've been trying to figure that out. Okay, tell me why you want this job.'

'Because it's everything I want to do with my life!' I said angrily, getting more frustrated than ever. 'Why do we have to do this now? The interview is thirteen minutes away.'

'We don't have to do this now, but please let me finish. I promise I won't say anything that's not helpful.' You grabbed my hand and placed in on the gear stick, under yours.

I took quick breaths, trying to calm myself. I felt like I was going to break down crying. It's only been a few months since we graduated, but there was so much pressure on me to find what I wanted to do for the rest of my life. I clearly wasn't handling it too well. 'Okay,' I whispered.

'This sounds like a good job. It definitely wouldn't hurt to have an offer from them; always good to have options. But I've known you for years, ever since you started to actively think about what you want to be doing with your life ... and babe, this isn't it. That doesn't mean that this couldn't be a great first job, something to have to bring you confidence, money, stability, shut up the neighbours ... whatever else is the immediate need. But at best, this is something you do while you chase your dreams. This is not the dream,' you said, squeezing the hand you held under yours. 'It's not *your* dream.'

I thought about that for a minute. You knew me so well ... even better than I knew myself. I finally voiced my insecurities. 'What if ... I never achieve my dreams? What if this is the best I can do?' I said quietly, even as my body relaxed and my breathing began to return to normal, because you were there – touching me, listening to me, calming me down.

You laughed. 'Seriously? I know you tend to exaggerate and it's one of the things that I love about you, but this is ridiculous, even for you. You finished college three months ago. There's all the time in the world. All we have to do is start somewhere and we'll build on it till we get to the dream part. Rome wasn't built in a day, and all that. They were right. But also, look at this job objectively. It's not your dream. You're good at lists – make lists of things this job offers and what you really, really want. Compare the overlap. There's very little.'

'How do you know this?' I asked, genuinely confused.

'Because I know you,' you said simply.

I thought about it. Sitting next to you in the car, in the last few minutes before we reached the office, I thought about what the job offered and what I wanted, and how it didn't really align with my plan at all. 'I got so caught up with finding a job, any job, that I stopped thinking about what I wanted. That was moved to the bottom of my list of priorities.'

'Of course you have a list of priorities.' You chuckled.

I snatched my hand back and pushed your arm lightly. 'So, what do we do about this interview?' I asked.

'We go in and blow their minds. Ask yourself what *they* have to offer *you*, not only all the things you can do for them. This isn't life or death. This is great practice for the real jobs. If you get an offer, we can think about our next steps then. Nothing to lose.'

'Nothing to lose,' I repeated.

That had become my mantra for every job I applied for after that interview. I never got an offer for that job though, but it didn't bother me as much as it would've without your inputs.

But this job … this is the one I really want. It's the perfect balance of everything I want to do and learn. It hits the most points on my checklist. I'm worried that I blew the interview, but we'll find out soon. I wished you were there to calm me down before I walked into that interview. I don't know how that had become your job. But I liked how you took it on without complaints. You were my anchor in the little storms I seem to face constantly in my life. You grounded me when I was all over the place…

I wish you were here.

October

Abhay,

You have to know that, under normal circumstances, I would never do this. If you were in love with Simran, and she was in love with you, and both of you were happy together, I would never send you this letter. In fact, I have written to you several times over this past year, and kept the letters hidden in a folder on my computer, never to be discovered. I could never bring myself to send you those. They were obsessive and repetitive, circular — like my thoughts.

They helped me though. Sometimes, when I feel unsettled and I don't know what's causing that feeling, I write. I write whatever's going on, whatever I feel, and I speculate. I call it writing therapy. Because when I go back to the page and read what I'd written, it helps clarify things in my head. I wrote to you every once in a while. These letters, I never sent you, but they were like a friend ... a safe place where I could share things.

I found out last week that Simran and you broke up. I don't want to assume that I was part of the reason why, but I have to believe that I played some minor role in this happening. I feel terrible about this. I hope you two didn't end on terrible terms, or get hurt. But knowing how love works, that's probably too much to hope for.

You don't have to tell me what happened with Simran. We don't have to talk about her and your relationship at all. That is not the reason I'm writing to you.

The reason I'm writing to you ... is because, Abhay, I'm in love with you. I have loved you for as long as I've known you, and in this past year, no matter how many times I have tried to deny that, even to myself, I have failed.

I can't stop thinking about you. Leaving you, making that decision ... was hard. But it wasn't the hardest thing I've had to do. That would be ... staying away from you. When every fibre in my body revolted against it, unwilling to accept a life without you, I still kept telling myself that it was okay, I was okay. But I wasn't. I'm not okay.

Wasn't it supposed to get easier and easier every day? To be away from you, and stay away from you? I was supposed to get used to it. Continue living, as if a part of me wasn't missing. I couldn't do it. I can't do it, Abhay. Please don't make me live without you, because that life sucks. I don't want it.

Is it too late? Do we still have a chance? For months, I told myself that this was the right decision, and slowly, we'll reverse the damage, life would be normal again. I thought that if I set a path for myself, consciously wrote down my steps and followed them through, my head could guide me, one day at a time, till enough time passed, and I could begin to let my heart make decisions for me again.

Turns out, it doesn't work like that. My entire being revolted against this decision my head made. Leaving you that day, and then staying away from you every day ... every single day away from you has been miserable. A special kind of hell I've built for myself.

These letters I've been writing to you every month, they're full of thought spirals that are often obsessive and do not make any sense. But somehow they keep me grounded. It feels as though through these words, I've been tracking my progress since the breakup. Most of it probably doesn't make sense, but I'd hoped that it would eventually get to a point where my words would start making more and more sense ... as I approach sanity.

Life still feels pretty insane. I'm discarding my plan for life. My brain doesn't get to make decisions for me anymore. The more I try to be in control, the more control I lose. Deciding to be without you and move on didn't work. No matter how hard I tried, it just didn't work. So, I should let my instincts guide me, right? I don't know what to do anymore. Nothing else works.

If I had to, could I live without you? Yes. I would be unhappy for a while, but I wouldn't die. With time, things would get better, and I would move on eventually. But do I want that? No. I don't want a life without you. I'm willing to risk everything again, wear my heart on my sleeve and dive into this with you again. I'm choosing to love you. Will you choose me too?

Abhay, I'm still in love with you. I always have been, and it looks like I always will be. No matter how hard I try to deny it, I know how my heart really feels. I come up with these elaborate plans, the reasons why we don't work, the reasons why we shouldn't be together. Sometimes, it feels like there are so many. At other times, no matter how hard I try, I can't think of even one. Not one reason why we shouldn't be together.

I know, it sounds crazy, because so much time has passed, I did something terrible to you when I ran away without explanation. You'll probably never be able to trust me again, we will probably never be able to build the trust again, to get to a point where we're not broken anymore. Then there's family, and friends ... they're still getting used to the idea of us not being together. There's so much bitterness between our families since the breakup ... I don't know if that can ever be fixed. I don't know where we would even begin.

Biggest of all: *you*. How do you feel? Do you still love me too? Do you think you can try to give me another chance? Do you think we can go back to the way things were before?

This is such a shot in the dark, but if I don't take this chance, I know I will always regret it. I love you, Abhay. And I want to be with you. I want to work with you, to put together all of the broken pieces of us ... make us whole again.

The first thing that comes to mind, the one you pointed out, the incident with ... that girl. I don't want to say her name. It's inconsequential to our lives. I will try to explain to you to the best of my abilities what that one incident did to me. Maybe then we can try to work on fixing things, if you still love me...

When I first met you, I fell in love with you as instantly as you fell in love with me. We were so different from each other, but there was this undeniable chemistry. We had the most random things in common. Even though our personalities were exact opposite of each other's, as we got to know each other, we realized that we were more alike than different.

Deep down, we have the same values. We live by the same principles. We have the same definitions of right and wrong. But all of that we discovered later. In the beginning, all I saw were differences.

You were outgoing, with a big, happy personality that shone through in any room. You took over any space you were in. No one could ignore you; you were never a part of the background. When I got to know you, I found out that you were patient and kind. And also kind of a jerk when you needed to be. I liked that. You took shit from no one. You were confident, always knew exactly what you wanted and went for it.

When I first met you, I wasn't the most social being. I liked to be left alone with my books. I liked to read, spend time thinking about things, hang out with my friends. I liked listening to music, looking for meaning in words. I didn't care that I was a cliché. I was happy with my small existence. I was so anxious inside, wanted such big things from life. I didn't have the time or energy to impress others, and I never felt the need to do that either.

Now that I think about it, I realize that you were always more of a businessman. You set out to seek what you wanted, and always won. Driven, focused, sure. You never hesitated, never questioned anything. You weren't crippled by doubt or uncertainty. You decided your own path, and made sure things went your way.

I, on the other hand, was always more of an artist ... one without a form of art. I drew, but not very often. I spent time with ideas – reading books, watching films, having conversations with close friends. From my first job, I've established that I like to create. That's what makes me feel productive and brings me fulfilment at the end of the day. Coming up with ideas for campaigns, creating content of all kinds for different platforms, engaging audiences in our narrative – that's what I thrive on.

If our jobs say anything about our personalities, it's clear that you're the person who single-mindedly sets out to reach goals. I'm always looking for more ... what else can we be doing, how to get more people to engage with us, raise more awareness. I'm not saying that your life is easier ... just that mine's messy. My head is always full of flying fragments of thoughts and ideas, I'm always working towards something.

You grounded me. When we were together, you were my pillar. As I lived my life stumbling from one idea to another, you were the only constant thing that brought me happiness, loved me when I needed it, shook me out of my own self-dug holes whenever necessary. I depended on you.

I showed you all of me, gave you my everything. You became my everything. I couldn't imagine a life without you.

So, when one day, after all we'd been through, you presented me with this information that went against everything I had ever known to be true ... my mind could not process it. I could not believe that you would do that. To me, when you knew you were my everything.

If this new piece of information was true, everything else that I had ever believed in was a lie. These truths could not exist together. They simply did not belong in the same world.

The world under my feet shifted. I questioned everything you'd ever said to me. Everything I'd felt. Everything I believed you felt towards me ... it was all a lie. I couldn't pick and choose based on what I wanted the reality to be. I couldn't assume that you meant one thing, but maybe not that other thing. You meant nothing. All of it was a lie. I was betrayed by the one person I shared everything with. Someone I thought I knew better than I knew myself. If I couldn't believe in you anymore, I lost trust in myself, and the world.

Maybe it's that blind first-love thing. I gave you my all, without questions. I never doubted anything, just put all my faith in you, until one day everything changed and I forgot how to think or be anymore.

How could you do that to me, Abhay? How could you even think about someone else? I knew that we had problems. It wasn't the easiest time for either of us. Things were rough at home. You had started working for your dad's company, and that took a lot from you. I couldn't find a good job, and that was taxing. After college ended, we had less and less in common. Our lives were very different now.

I know all of this. I know how hard it was. Somewhere along the way, as we grew, we grew apart.

It was painful, and disappointing. I missed you, I was unhappy ... but not once during all of this did I think about someone else. It was never that bad. Our love was still very real. Maybe the romance had faded a little, maybe we weren't as carefree and happy anymore. But we still loved each other, didn't we?

Then how could you kiss that girl, Abhay? Why? You say that it was just a mistake, and I want to believe you.

I want to believe you so badly... But then I remember how I felt the night you told me about her, and all of those terrible memories come back to me...

We tried to move on from it. Admittedly, we did a terrible job at it. You were right, we should've resolved the problem before moving on. But working on a resolution required addressing the problem. It was too real ... I couldn't handle it. I was too weak. I couldn't bear the thought of you with someone else, so I wanted to pretend it never happened. I couldn't talk to you about it, dissect everything, relive it...

Our relationship was perfect from the beginning. From day 1, things had come easy for us. We'd found each other young, and put our faith in each other without any conditions or scepticism. I didn't want to accept that we were not perfect. Or that a mistake was made that could destroy everything. So I ignored it.

That didn't work either. Ignoring it, pretending it never happened was taking its toll on me. For the first time in my adult life, you weren't in it with me. I was in this alone. I refused to let you in, because you were the source of the pain. You did this to me, and I was angry. I didn't want to give you the satisfaction of having helped ease the pain. Very stubborn and irrational of me, I know. And it cost me dearly.

We were acting as if everything was normal, but I found myself questioning everything that came out of your mouth after that. Or anyone's mouth. What if everyone was lying to everyone else all the time? All you can do is trust that people are honest ... you can't always know for sure. Then how can you trust anyone fully, ever?

That incident planted a seed of uncertainty in my head. It refused to be squashed. It kept growing and growing till I believed nothing and no one. And every little thing that went wrong in our lives after that added to this pile of issues.

When everything with our families started happening — the arguments, cold wars, the drama — and you seemed unbothered, that added to it. When you made new friends at work and didn't have as much time for me anymore, that added to it. When I couldn't figure out what I wanted in my career, that added to it. When I woke up from terrible nightmares and couldn't tell anyone or seek help, that added to it. When everyone planned out the rest of our lives for us without our inputs and I felt unable to breathe, that added to it.

It piled up. All of it, together, it was too much for me to take. Without you, I found myself terribly inadequate to handle all that. And while you were so close to me, you were also farther away than you'd ever been. Then one day, I broke.

I have lived with you in my life, and I have lived without you. Nothing is worth a life without you, Abhay. I know we have problems. Big problems. Re-establishing trust on both sides, that's a tall order. But if you still love me as much as I love you, we owe ourselves another chance. Please, please give me another chance.

What do you think? Are you where I am? Or am I making a complete fool of myself by saying all of these things right now? I don't mind; as long as there's even a one per cent chance that we can fix this, I'm happy to be the fool.

I want to build a life with you. I want everything back. I want to be by your side, and love you and care for you. I want your kisses, I want your arm around my back, I want your shoulder. I want your voice in my ear in the morning, the softness of your hair, your hand in mine. I want conversations and understanding and truths and challenges. I want us back. Please, please tell me I'm not too late.

When you get this letter, please don't rush to a decision. Please give it time. If you decide something now, but then go back on a decision once you've had time to think about it, I don't think my heart can take it. I'll wait for your letter, but please only write to me when you are certain.

One way or another, no matter what happens, please know that I will always cherish our time together and remember our moments fondly. When I think of you, I will never let my heart grow bitter. I believe that you truly loved me. Maybe we've lost it, maybe we haven't ... but no one can take away the time that we spent together. I will always have that. Maybe that can be enough. Maybe I can convince myself that it was enough.

But Abhay, from the deepest corners of my heart ... I hope that it's not too late.

Nidhi

November

Dear Nidhi,

When you left, a lot of things changed for me too. You would understand this — it was quite similar to your description of how you felt when I told you about that kiss. My entire world-view shifted.

Like you, I also shared my everything with you. I told you everything about myself, opened myself up to you completely, put my faith in you. And one day, you decided you didn't want to be with me anymore. You left, without giving me a reason. I wondered, for weeks and months, I thought through everything I have ever done, everything I'd said to you, every second I spent with you, trying to pinpoint where things went wrong, why you left me.

I was completely blindsided. I never saw it coming. Even after you drove away, right in front of my eyes, it took me a while to realize what had happened. The one person I put before everyone else, including myself, suddenly didn't want anything to do with me. You disappeared. No explanation. Not even so much as a text message.

You would understand how, after that, it's really hard to trust you, or anyone.

Everything changed around me. At home, outside with friends or at work, everywhere I went, people would look at me with pity. I was given preferential treatment. I resented that. I stopped talking to people, just to avoid having to answer how I was doing.

I was not doing well, Nidhi. I thought about you all the time. There wasn't a minute that went by without me thinking about you. I didn't know where you were, what you were doing. I didn't know why you'd left, or if you were coming back. I didn't know if you were okay, if you needed me.

I missed you so much. I was looking forward to spending a lifetime with you. And then you were just gone. I don't know where, or why. You just threw everything away and left me.

Days went by really slowly. Sometimes I would hear from someone about you leaving or coming back, or something one of your relatives said. I didn't know what to believe and what not to believe. I couldn't trust anything.

I called you every day. Every single day, for weeks. I must've left a hundred messages. I didn't get a word back from you. Do you have any idea how that feels? Having the door shut on your face like that?

These letters you speak of ... where are they? You say that you've been thinking about me, but to me, from where I stand, you walked away and never looked back. For ten months. You were completely okay. You never missed me, never even asked me how I was doing. So, when you speak about us being miles away, that's exactly how I feel too. I never got a hint that you were still thinking about me. I never stopped loving you. I desperately wanted to be with you, but you were ... fine.

You were okay. With your new job and positive outlook on life ... rationalizing everything, finding reason, setting your path and following it. It seemed like you knew exactly what you wanted. Even when we met back in March and talked things over, not once did you express any kind of interest in our relationship. No remorse. You didn't miss me at all, or wished things were different. It was already in the past for you. You had already moved on.

After that, finally getting some answers, and seeing for myself that your resolve was final, that was when I decided that it was time for me to move on too. I couldn't be hung up on you forever. I had to stop waiting and hoping for things to go back to what I used to think was normal. I had to let you go, because you had already left me.

I started to take more interest in my work, distracting myself with it. I never stopped thinking about you, and I didn't try. I knew when I first fell in love with you that if it ever ended, it would break me. I knew you were trouble. I knew I would be left heartbroken. I knew what I was getting into from the word go.

I wanted to think that it was getting better each day, but that's not what it felt like. I had good days and bad. Sometimes I would go an entire week without missing you. Some days it took all my energy just to get out of the bed in the morning.

When I met Simran, I felt something. For the first time in months, I felt as if my life wasn't over. That I might have a shot at finding something meaningful again. You probably don't want to hear this, but I have to be honest with you. I tried really, really hard with her. In the light of recent events, it's clear that I wasn't doing a good job at it, but I gave it all I had. I just didn't have enough to give her.

I consciously told myself to not let my past direct my present, and so, when I met her, I tried to trust her. I tried to give her whatever I had, but it was never enough. No matter how much I tried, it wouldn't make a difference. She was always dissatisfied with me, and it wasn't her fault. She deserved much, much more than I had to give to her. A full person would have been much more open, more loving and caring. He would've paid her more attention, been more available.

No matter what I did, it was never enough. And that's a slippery slope. I hated making her feel like she wasn't good enough. Or that she was doing something wrong, and if she would change something about herself, she could fix things. That's a terrible place to be. I didn't want her to feel like that. She wasn't doing anything wrong. She was great, honestly. She cared about me, she was always sweet and kind, which is why it killed me to see what I was doing to her.

This reminds me of that thing you used to say about guys calling their exes crazy. Maybe it's the guys who make their exes kind of crazy? When there's an imbalance in the amount of love two people have for each other, the person who loves more always suffers. Because they give their all to the other person, but never get the same amount in return. Which makes them wonder if they're doing something wrong, and the harder they try, the worse it gets. Situations like this can spiral out of control.

When I saw what I was doing to Simran, I had to end it. My inadequacies were affecting her, turning her into this insecure person... She wasn't happy, and it was all my doing. When I realized that, I knew that we couldn't be together anymore, which is why I initiated the breakup.

You're right in assuming that you had something to do with it. You were part of the reason. You were in her head, and mine, and you were very much present in our lives and relationship. But even without you, I would still not be with her, because she deserves much more. I felt inadequate, and I made her feel inadequate.

Also, because I was still in love with you. I *am* still in love with you. I don't know how to not love you; I don't think I'm capable of doing that.

When you talk about giving us another chance, I want to forget every bad thing that happened and run to you. I've dreamed about holding you again, kissing you. I never thought we would get another chance. But then I remember ... how easily you left me and what it did to me. If you did it once, how can I be sure you won't do it again?

Nidhi, I'm really sorry for all the terrible things I put you through. If I could go back and take it back, I would. You know that. I hope you know that. It meant nothing to me, that kiss was nothing. You have to believe me. You say you can't trust me anymore, and that you think that everything I've said to you is a lie, but if you'd just give me another chance, I will show you that I mean all of it.

The kiss was a mistake. I regret it deeply. I wish it hadn't happened, I wish I had stopped it. I wish I hadn't hurt you so badly, I wish I hadn't broken your trust. When you tell me about your loss of faith in people, your constant scepticism, your nightmares ... it kills me. I would do anything to make it better for you. I will spend the rest of my life earning your trust.

I can't undo the past, but if you let me, I will prove to you how much I love you and care about you. There's nothing I wouldn't do for you.

But Nidhi, just as you lost faith in me after the kiss, I lost faith in you too ... when you threw away our entire relationship and left me. You're right in saying that maybe we never faced a real problem in our relationship before this, but I had always thought that when the problems did come, we would be able to recover from anything, together.

That we would fix it. We wouldn't throw it away.

But you did. You discarded everything we had and left. So, while every cell in my body wants to run to you and hold you and never let you go again, I'm also certain that if you left me again, I won't recover. If I trust you again, and fall deeper in love with you, and you leave me again...

We are worth fighting for. When we come to that, I will always choose fight. But if I choose fight, you cannot choose flight. You cannot run away. You cannot leave me again. So, when you say you want me back, when you make promises to me again, please make sure you only do that if you intend to keep them. You can't play with me. You can't be in this half-heartedly. If you're not sure, don't give me false hope.

This time, it has to be forever. Any problems that come our way, big or small, you have to promise to let me in. You have to let me help you. It's okay to take your time doing that, just as long as you give me a chance before making a drastic, life-changing decision for the both of us.

I will do anything for you. I'm not just saying that, Nidhi. Anything. To make you happy, to keep you happy. But I will also make mistakes. I'm human, I don't claim to be perfect. I will mess up, repeatedly. It's just who I am. No matter how hard I try, I know things will not always go as planned. There will be obstacles, I will be an idiot, I will do stupid things. But when I mess up, all you have to do is tell me to stop being a jerk, and I will. All you have to do is ask. I'll do anything.

Please, no more secrets. No more living in solitude and suffering in silence. I can't bear the thought of you going through what you did for months, while I was right there, oblivious to it all. I can't even imagine what it must've been like for you. I hate that I wasn't there to help you when you needed me the most. You have to let me in.

I promise not to make irreversible mistakes. I promise never to break your trust again, never to do anything that would make you question the faith you put in me. Every single day, I will wake up to prove to you that I love you, and I care about you more than anything else in the world, and that you can trust me. I promise to be yours forever, if you promise to be mine.

A lifetime. This time, it's for a lifetime.

So, if you're still unsure, if there's even a small grain of doubt in your mind about us, please, I beg you, please don't come back to me.

If you do come back to me, the only way we can move on from the past is by forgetting the cheating and abandoning. (Too soon? I thought it was funny, sorry.) We have to forgive each other for our betrayals and trust each other again, with everything we have. Without an ounce of doubt. It may sound unreasonable, probably even impossible, but just try. Just try to let go. It feels good, to not carry all of that on your shoulders anymore. All that stuff that slows us down, makes us sceptical about everything ... it feels good to get rid of that.

Most importantly, I want to tell you that I love you. I never stopped loving you, not for one second. Every single day, in everything I did, there was you. You never left me. You were in my heart, and I know that's one place you'll always be, no matter what happens in the rest of the world.

I want to wake up next to you. I want to bury my face in your hair, I want to kiss your neck. I want to get used to the twitch of your lips. I want to hold you, and never let you go again.

Please, let me be yours, for the rest of our lives. Please put your faith in me again. I want to build a life with you, I want to be by your side and have you by my side, ready to face whatever comes our way. Quite honestly, none of this is worth it, without you to share it with. No matter what I do, there's no meaning to any of it, not without you.

You are my everything. Please come back to me. Put your faith in us. We'll make it this time.

I love you.

Abhay

December

My dearest Abhay,

Let me start this letter by saying that this is super dumb. We've been back together two whole weeks, and you're sitting in the same room as me as I type this, so really, there is no need for me to type this, but fine, stop giving me the stink eye. I'm doing what you want. You win.

Speaking of winning, I haven't been doing that a lot recently, have I? The crazy part about that is that I don't even care. I like losing to you. At least for now, since it's so new (again) but I'm sure it'll get old real soon and things will get more competitive around here.

So, coming to the point — I'm writing this letter to promise you that I will never leave you (again) and this time I will keep my promise. In all seriousness, I know what I did was terrible. I realize what it must've taken for you to trust me again. So, this time, when I promise you that I will always love you, I mean it. When I tell you that I will never leave your side, I will always be with you, I will fight with you, no matter what happens,

I mean it more than I have ever meant anything in my life. I'm not exaggerating.

I'm trusting you and giving my all to you again. I know you will take care of it. And I will take care of you.

Thank you, for giving me another chance. When you showed up at my door with your letter ... my heart has never been so full. I would've been more nervous when you told me that I had to read the letter to find out your answer, but that stupid grin on your face gave it all away. You were never very good at keeping secrets, were you? (If you EVER try to cheat on me, please know that *I will know*. Please also know that I will find you, and I will kill you).

Anyway, so that day, as you grinned stupidly at me, I read your letter, rushing through it, but also wanting to slow down and savour every single word. Once the tears started flowing down my face, it became harder to read. Seeing that, you came closer to me. You held me from behind and read the letter with me.

And then I was crying too much and couldn't see at all, so you had to take over and read the rest of the letter to me while you held and comforted me. Thanks for that. You da best. Jk. But no, seriously, you rock. (Get it? Because you literally rocked me back and forth like a child to make me stop crying).

Okay, sorry. Just tryna keep it light.

I'm glad you came to me with the letter that day. After reading it, I definitely wouldn't have had the patience and self-control to sit down and respond thoughtfully. I would've just run to you. You probably would have sent me back and asked me to write this to you first. Seriously, why am I doing this again? It's almost 2018. Who writes letters?

To wrap this up, I want to make some promises to you that I intend to keep. I will always, always tell you when something goes wrong. I won't suffer in silence. I won't shut you out. I won't keep things from you and be passive-aggressive. I might be aggressive sometimes, but when I am aggressive, please try to remember that that is what you wanted. This is literally what you asked for and I have written proof. So, I'll tell you exactly how it is. You can count on that.

I promise that I will never run away. I will work with you to resolve any problems that come our way. I will fight for us. I won't give up that easy again. I will have faith in us, I will trust that nothing can be big enough to break us. We are a team. We are together in this. I will always remember that.

I will trust you completely. Like I did when I was nineteen. For this part, I'm going to be extra cheesy and share with you this poem (don't laugh) I wrote for you:

NINETEEN

It's a privilege
to fall in love
again
as if we were nineteen

To love
without conditions
baggage or reservations
trust issues and toxic scepticism

To be nineteen again,
a little crazy,
a lot stupid,
with an open heart

To be with someone
who makes you forget
all that's gone wrong
all that's broken

To love someone
with all we have
to love again
as if we were nineteen

Because we broke it once, this time we're being
extra careful. That doesn't mean that it's fragile. It's not

fragile. If anything, we're stronger than ever. We can overcome a lot, but if there was one good thing that came out of this past year of misery, it is the knowledge that what we have is precious. That we have to work on it every day, because it deserves our attention. After all is said and done, the love we share is the only thing we have that matters. And I promise you that I will always love you and cherish what we have.

So there, these are my promises to you. I'm promising you love, honesty, loyalty, fight, trust, compassion, care and so so much more love. I'm promising you a lifetime. I'm promising you all of me, for always.

Hugs, kisses and a whole lot of dirty stuff,

Nidhi

PS: How cheesy was I on a scale of 1 to 10?

*

My dearest Nidhi,
Finally. Thank you for that. I am keeping this in a safe place in case you forget any of this and try to pull one over me.

From this letter (whenever you stopped making jokes for two seconds and got serious) I can tell that you are still very wisdom-ous. Your wise-ness shines through. Love the poem (seriously) and also the general cheesiness of the letter was well received.

Let's hug, kiss and do a whole lot of dirty stuff,

Abhay

Epilogue

Nidhi's list of promises:

- I will always give you an accurate estimate of how long it's going to take me to get dressed. However, you must note that sometimes when I decide to do my hair, I genuinely do not know how long it might take. And it's not a lie if I'm not in on it. It's an inaccurate estimate. Not a lie.

- I will try to remember dates. Please note that I'm saying try. I can't promise that I'll remember all dates, all the time. I realize that it makes you unhappy that I forgot that today is exactly one year since we got back together. Yes, it's sweet that it matters to you and you care so much. But also, you have to know that just because dates don't hold special meaning to me, doesn't mean events don't either. I'll always remember the moments we shared on that day, but maybe not always remember the exact date. For you though, I will try.

- I will always play the devil's advocate. I will question things, and challenge your ideas, because we both thrive on that.

- I will not watch *Orange Is the New Black* without you. I'm sorry that I did that one time. But I won't watch a new episode without you, no matter how curious I get.

133

- I will always share my Uber status with you. You probably shouldn't worry so much, but yeah, okay, I'll share my Uber status with you.
- I won't run away when we get engaged again for realz this time next week.

*

Abhay's list of promises:

- I will not, on purpose, touch your knees, because I know it tickles and you don't like it. However, you must note that accidents happen, and oftentimes situations in life aren't a hundred per cent under my control.
- When we get engaged again next week, and you don't run away this time, I promise to let the guards at the door go … and not hire them again for our wedding.
- I promise to read first drafts of everything you write and give you my honest advice. Even when you write your first book, I promise to not spare your feelings and be brutally honest about what I think of your pages.
- I also promise that afterwards, I'll take you out for ice cream and make you feel better.
- I promise to always make you laugh. No matter what the situation is. (Even if it's a funeral, doesn't matter. You'll be the weirdo sniggering in the corner.)
- I promise to always, always love you.

Author's note

This book was hard to write. It wasn't planned. Usually, when I write, I have a plan in my head before I start; I know what's going to happen. I don't know *everything* that's going to happen, but I'm aware of the highlights and turning points. So, when I started writing this book without a plan, it was a new kind of challenge for me (I like to be able to control things, especially things I create).

I was only sure of one thing: Nidhi. I *knew* the character. Not in a creepy way, but what I mean is, when I was writing, I was completely inside her head. I knew how she felt, how she would react to situations, what she would and wouldn't do. Nidhi's circular thoughts, her confused feelings, her insecurities reflect the artist in her. (Maybe she'll be a writer one day. Who knows!)

With these letters, I tried to understand the reasons why people fall in love, the reasons why they stay together, the reasons they break up. I tried to explore what happens when two people who love each other deeply ... break. And what it takes for them to find their way back to each other.

Admittedly, I didn't know that they were going to get back together. But as I wrote about them, I couldn't see how Nidhi would be truly happy without Abhay. And

Abhay, even though we don't see in detail how he's feeling throughout the year, needs Nidhi just as much as she needs him, if not more. Something essential connects them, and neither of them can be themselves without the other. When they grew up (graduated from college and stepped into the real world) they grew apart. Everything in their lives pulled them away from each other, till they broke. But their reason to be together (love) ultimately outweighed the challenges.

Love sometimes just happens. However, most times, it needs constant care and attention. People tend to forget that, start taking things for granted, make mistakes, break trust – be generally careless idiots. I wanted to see what happens after a break like that, where both people broke each other's trust in a way they believed was irreparable.

Another thing that was an interesting challenge was this format: letters. We don't see things the way they happen, but we see them through one person's eyes. We get confused when she is confused. Her reality is the only reality, because we only have that one perspective.

In the end, they *choose* to come back to each other. The separation was hard on both of them, but with time, they would've been fine without the other person in their lives. But they chose love, they chose to work on their issues, rebuild their relationship and ultimately create a bond much stronger than one they shared before. They developed emotional resilience, and are more prepared to face problems in the future. Their connection is not fragile, or something that can easily be swayed, because they're more realistic now, while still remaining romantic, and they value what they share more than ever, because they've lost it once.

And that's what I wanted to write about – the idea that people have about a 'perfect love' and how they react when it's tarnished. Rebuilding trust, taking second chances, risking heartbreak again – all of it requires a lot of courage. But ultimately, for Nidhi and Abhay, their love is worth all of it.

Acknowledgements

I'm going to do this in the sequence of actual quantitative help I've received for this book from the amazing people in my life. Anish Chandy (my agent and first reader) for giving the manuscript some very necessary hate, which freaked me out, and then made this a better book. Ananth Padmanabhan (CEO, HarperCollins) for coming up with the concept for *Letters* and swooping in whenever needed to save the day. Laura Duarte Marston (first non-publishing person to read *Letters*) for your overwhelmingly positive feedback and constant love and support in life in general. Nick Sheridan (second non-publishing person to read *Letters*) for your unique perspective, attention to detail and OCD tendencies that match mine. Nejla Asimovic (soul sister) for intense conversations about life and purpose; I'd be lying if I said Nidhi's character isn't at least partially inspired by you. Sandra-Meijer-Polak (best friend) and Yannick Meijer (best friend's husband) for long brainstorming phone calls and being my family away from home, apart from being very cool people, of course. Prerna Gill (editor, HarperCollins) for your hard work on the manuscript and unlimited patience with missed deadlines.

Mother, father, brother, extended family, friends. You know your contribution; please feel free to claim credit accordingly. Big hugs.